GATHERING

BY:

ERIC GARDNER

A Thirteenth Legion Series Novel

Gathering

Copyright © 2017 Eric Gardner

All rights reserved. No part of this book may be used or reproduced by any means, graphic, electronic, or mechanical, including photocopying, recording, taping or by any information storage retrieval system without the written permission of the publisher except in case of brief quotations embodied in critical articles and reviews.

This is a work of fiction. All of the characters, names, incidents, organizations, and dialogue in this novel are either the products of the author's imagination or are used fictitiously.

ISBN-13:978-1545466582

ISBN-10:1545466580

All quotations from existing biblical works come from Holy Bible NIV (New International Version.)

All quotations from existing biblical works come from Holy Bible NIV (New International Version.) Quotations from The Book of Enoch originate from R.H. Charles' translation.

The book of Maccabees is quoted from the Jerusalem Bible.

Author Photo Taken by Heidi Schranz

Cover Photograph by Dietmar Rabich Wikimedia Commons / "Lüdinghausen, Burg Lüdinghausen - 2014 -- 5500-2" / CC BY-SA 4.0.

For my wife.

In all things you are my better half; what a wild and unpredictable road we have been on. I can only dream of where our lives will go together next.

This is a work of fiction...

Acknowledgments

John and Lois, thank you for always pushing me ever onward.

Books of the Thirteenth Legion Series

Book 1- Defiance

Book 2- Awakening

Book 3- Sacrifice

Book 4- Gathering

Book 5- Descent
(Sumer 2017)

Book 6- Vengeance
(Fall 2017)

What if your understanding of the world was misleading? What if your beliefs had been manipulated? Not out of malice, but out of the need for humanity to have free will. If mankind truly understood what lurked in the darkness, all of the souls of the earth would flock to a savior; but is that a true measure of faith? Throughout the ages, the Morning Star has woven a nearly impenetrable web of lies and falsehoods. Compounding history's truth is humanity's good intentions to maintain the grand design for how the world sees creation. Our eyes have been kept from the truth. For those chosen souls, the secrets of the universe will unravel. The web of the devil will be torn away, and the incomprehensible truth will be revealed. Is your soul marked by the heavens to be among the saints of His legion?

If so, welcome to the Thirteenth Legion.

Welcome to the war!

GATHERING

Acknowledgments i

Previous Pivotal Personalities vii

A word to the reader ix

Till Death Do Us Part 1

There are Always Eyes in the Shadows 7

You Never Plan to Fail—You Only Fail to Plan 10

Evil has Many Names—Those That Serve It Have but One...Damned 19

There is Never Any Time for Reflection 30

No Good Deed Goes Unpunished 36

Everyone has a Purpose—For Some, it is Dual-Fold 41

The Questions Will Need an Answer 47

The Truth Will Set You Free—But to What End? 52

A Foretold Meeting 56

You Think Selling Your Soul to the Devil is Bad—Try Holding a Meeting with Him 62

Every Footstep We Take on Our Own is One Farther Away from the Father of Creation 71

Timely Assistance 76

Whatever Action I Take, let it be for the Greater Glory of God! 82

By My Own Hand 87

Motives Unclear 90

Each Path Given to Us from the Creator is Unique 94

Each of Us is a Spark in the Darkness—Who will See Us Before We Fade into Nothingness? 101

Closest of Advisors 104

Essentials 108

The Enemy of my Enemy is Never my Friend 116

Sweat in Training so as Not to Bleed in Combat 124

Hidden in Plain Sight 129

Have Faith 133

Those Who Tell Secrets from the Past Bear More Than Just the Tales They Tell 139

Truth is Overrated in the House of the Damned 149

Evil Knows No Limits 152

If Knowledge is Power, How Powerful are Those Who Hold the Truths Behind the Knowledge? 160

Man has Always Feared the darkness. 168

Why Now are we so Unafraid of What Lurks in the Shadows? 168

Corruption of the Flesh Leads to Corruption of the Mind 173

Previous Pivotal Personalities

Gabriel Willis: Simply trying to save his family from a demented cult, he is pulled into an unending battle between good and evil. Now he must safe guard the very woman he planned on using to secure the release of his wife and children.

Othia Morgan: An archeologist whose recent discovery will never be shared with the world, is running for her life. Trusting Gabriel, she must circumnavigate the globe to reach their goal and obtain a treasure meant to aid humanity in the war to come.

Samantha Famsic: Young and vibrant. The touch from an unholy messenger has awakened a dark spiritual gift in her that will allow the true spirit of anyone within sight to be revealed—that is, if her soul remains pure.

Stephen James: A seasoned police detective, he is on the hunt of a murderous cult. His only clue is a strange archaic symbol.

Uther Jander: Once a broken and fragile man, now powerful, ruthless, and corrupt. He heads the Assembled, a powerful group intent on ushering in his dark lord's new reign upon the earth. Black arts have allowed a windfall of fortunate successes that have placed him in influential positions, giving him control of vital areas within all major governments.

Cincaid: Cold, clean, methodical, and thorough. Uther's second, confidante, and expediter for all the dark deeds crafted and conducted by the cult. Beautiful and desirable, she thrives on the thrill of the hunt and the underlying inevitability of the kill. She has but one goal in her narrowly focused life: to please her master in every way possible.

CS: Cincaid's Scout is a woman of unique qualities. Not elevated among the ranks of the Assembled, she is still held in high regard and only given the most sensitive missions from her Mistress. Fanatical in her devotion, she never questions or complains. She does all things only for Cincaid's approval.

Semyaza: Seraph of the Twelfth Legion of Angels. Tasked by the Son to aid the Thirteenth Legion as they begin to prepare to battle the forces of evil.

Vicaro: Once the guardian of Eden, now his soul inhabits the sword Gabriel wields in battle. A symbiotic relationship is shared between both warriors.

A word to the reader

Gathering is the fourth book in the Thirteenth Legion series. *Sacrifice* showed us the final days of Gabriel and his group's journey to reach a location where they will undertake the monumental task of creating an army to combat the legions of the damned. Illuminated to this life-changing task in the mountains of Afghanistan, Gabriel, along with Othia and Samantha, traversed the globe by natural and supernatural means to arrive at Mount Deception in Washington state.

Epic battles between demonic monstrosities and angelic warriors allowed for the rescue of Gabriel's wife and children from The Estate, and Samantha from Purgatory. While these events transpired outside the public eye, Detective James unraveled a sadistic murder spree perpetrated by an elusive cult. The raw, violent nature of the crimes not only disturbed him and his team, but sent him across Washington State in search of the meaning of a symbol which linked all the horrific acts. The two groups came together at a hidden temple entrance where their paths were intertwined, and a sacrifice was taken from each of them.

The flip side of the coin is the group known as the Assembled. Uther and Cincaid have ushered a demonic envoy into humanities realm. Mrs. Gionel has been instructed to aid the clandestine organization but her ulterior motives have yet to be completely revealed. Even with employing multiple intelligence organizations from around the world, agents of the Assembled are still struggling to kill or capture Gabriel and his traveling companions.

Our story begins where we left our heroes and villains. Gabriel, Samantha, Othia and James have just entered the Stronghold Ephesus. Their time is short, for in less than two weeks the chosen souls amongst the world's population will begin to arrive. Not only does Gabriel need to grieve for the loss of his wife and son. He must prepare to win the hearts and minds of thousands of people he has never met.

Chapter 1

Till Death Do Us Part

He lifts up a banner for the distant nations, he whistles for those at the ends of the earth. Here they come, swiftly and speedily! Not one of them grows tired or stumbles, not one slumbers or sleeps; not a belt is loosened at the waist, not a sandal strap is broken–In that day they will roar over it like the roaring of the sea. And if one looks at the land, he will see darkness and distress...
~ Isaiah 5:26–30

Location: Denver, Colorado, U.S.A.

Blurred eyes glanced at the clock on the nightstand, and the blinking numbers on its digital face read 02:47. A frustrated sigh lingered in the darkness of the room as peaceful sleep once again failed to come. Frustrated, Scott sat up slowly, trying not to wake the beautiful woman lying next to him. Moonlight trickling in through the bay window shimmered on her golden hair.

He smiled to himself. His body ached as he stood and walked into the living room. Flares of pain from his tired joints retold him tales of never-ending labor and pleaded with him to return to the comfort of the bed he had just left. The dreams had come again. They had been a persistent fixture in his life for the last six months. Dreams of war, carnage and suffering plagued him constantly.

He tried to seek help at the request of his wife. Her concerned eyes compelled him to at least try to remedy whatever ailment was afflicting him. Nothing had worked. He felt this pull, that his life was supposed to monumentally change somehow and that he was avoiding his destiny by simply continuing to go to work each day on the construction crew. All the professionals he saw told him that his insomnia was unique. They all said it was a one-in-a-million affliction, and there truly was no cure. He would have to live with it or find a way to deal with the effects of a strong multidrug cocktail that would allow his body to shut down at night. He could still hear the pleas of his wife to try the medication, and he had honestly given it his best. One week into the treatment, he stopped. His reflexes had been slowed to the point that he couldn't function at work, and without his paycheck, they couldn't survive.

He sat down reluctantly on the couch, the last images of his most recent nightmare still fresh in his mind. His body tensed as he shut his eyes for a moment, fearful of returning to the hellish landscape he seemed destined to visit each night. As he looked around their modest living room, he sat in the darkness. The moonlight let him see enough to keep from falling over the furniture but allowed his body to relax somewhat and not feel compelled to turn on the television or read a book.

The dreams were the same every night. He found himself in an underground cavern, surrounded by others who seemed to share his affliction, and then he would be whisked away to a desolate landscape, rich colors of red and black swirling around in his mind. He would notice his feet sinking slowly into a dust like substance, and then the creatures would come—horrors that burned their images into his mind. He would wake just as his limbs were being torn from his body, his own blood covering his face.

During the first few weeks, he had literally jumped out of bed screaming, his wife frantically trying to calm him and reassure him that he was safe. Now the dreams merely drenched him with sweat and kept him awake. A perpetual half-sleep had plagued him for months. He placed his hands over his face and massaged his temples as he tried again to shut his eyes.

"Scott," an unknown voice whispered. Fear shot through his body, and he froze, his hands refusing to pull themselves from his eyes. "Scott—" With his eyes still closed, his body instinctively wanted him to run, to get off the couch and do something, *anything*, but his mind was so shocked and fear-stricken that he remained rooted to the cushions. He had heard the voice before during the first few nights of the dreams, telling him something—he couldn't remember what—but the fact that it was now coming to him when he was awake truly threatened to unravel his sanity.

"Open your eyes, Scott. We have much to discuss, and very little time to do it. I said open your eyes!" The room shook with the command, and Scott's hands shot to his sides, his eyes flaring open. He stared open-mouthed at a shimmering orb in front of him. A ball of pure white light had appeared. It seemed to be holding its brilliance back as it pulsed, almost as if it were aware of the darkness around it and didn't want to disturb it.

"What are you?" he asked in his thick New Jersey accent. A croaked whisper was all he could manage, his mind whirling, not truly comprehending what was going on and his body still pleading with him to move, run, get out of there somehow.

"It is time, Scott. You have seen what is to come. We have shown you how it will unfold in the future. You must stand to stem the tide, or all will be lost." Nothing was making any sense. He fought to sort it out. The light began to grow in intensity, and soon he had to shield his eyes from the blinding orb before him.

"This is not what is planned for you. Your fate is not here. You must stem the tide. You must defend that which is vital for our survival. Go now. Travel to Ephesus. You must heed the call—" The light faded rapidly and then was gone, the flashes of it were still visible when he shut his eyes.

"Scott, who are you talking to?" He turned and saw his wife standing in the doorway to their bedroom, looking sleepily at him.

Scott shook his head. "No one, babe. Just goin' a little nuts. I couldn't sleep again, so I'm just muttering to myself." His story seemed to alleviate any need for further explanation, and she smiled wearily and went back to bed.

A whispered rasp filled the living room again, and he shuddered. "Travel to the west. Seek the temple of Ephesus. Stem the tide, or all is lost. The dreams are real. You are in danger—" His heart jumped into his throat. He searched for a reasonable explanation. There had to be some way of rationalizing this.

He glanced back toward the bedroom and saw his wife still standing there, her nightgown bunching at an odd angle. With her face still covered in shadow, he couldn't tell if she was asleep standing up or just staring at him and waiting patiently for him to relinquish his wakeful state and join her in bed. Scott stood and stretched for a moment and then walked slowly to his wife leaning in the doorway of their bedroom. As he got closer, the shadows seemed to fade away, and his heart nearly stopped beating in his chest. His wife's body stood in the doorway covered in blood, her nightgown bunched at the center where a massive chunk of her stomach was missing, her hands keeping her intestines from falling to the floor.

"Help me. Help me—" Her voice began to chant the two words over and over, and each time, they echoed in the small apartment. Her body rocked back and forth as Scott reached out to grab her shoulders, his mind trying to find a way to stop the bleeding that was drenching the floor. When he touched her shaking shoulders, her eyes shifted to his, and she screamed. She lunged at him, her wet, bloody form slamming into him and sending them both to the floor. She thrashed on top of him, his hands slipping as her blood-covered limbs flailed around. A wave of warmth washed over him as her blood saturated his clothes.

His wife froze on top of him, and she looked at him through bloodshot eyes before she said, "Stem the tide. Save us. Please, Scott, save me—" Her slender form shook again violently, and then she was propelled backward as if pulled upright by an unseen force. She looked down at him with a sickening smile on her face. A wet sound filled his ears as he watched in frozen terror as his wife's blood soaked fingers tugged on her intestines. Then she pressed her delicate fingers into her wide eyes, spilling fountains of blood and gelatinous fluid onto his chest.

Her screams filled the house again, and he struggled to get up, his feet and hands slipping on the blood and fluids now covering the floor. His wife planted a foot squarely onto his chest and stared down at him through the dark cavities where her beautiful blue eyes had once resided. "Answer the call, Scott, or all is lost. Save us—"

A blinding flash of light seared his retinas, and when it cleared, he saw his wife's beautiful face staring at him with panic. "Honey, what's wrong? It's safe. You're okay. Honey, it is just a bad dream." Her soothing tone did little to diminish the mounting fear that was taking control of his body.

He could still smell the blood and gore from a few moments ago, and he couldn't shake the image of his wife's blood-covered body from his mind. She pulled him close and sobs racked his body. "What's wrong, babe? You're okay. It was just a dream." Scott was about to pull away from her soft frame when he heard a whisper just underneath her breath, "Answer the call. Or there will be so much pain. Help us, Scott."

He pushed back rapidly and saw the bloody form of his wife again, now holding outstretched arms, beckoning him toward her mutilated body. He blinked, and the image changed. Fear covered his wife's face, and she tried to pull him close again. Scott pushed her hands away and said, "We need to leave." She paused for a moment, not comprehending what he was saying. He stood and quickly pulled her to her feet. "Get your stuff. We need to leave now!"

A panic began to grow. He saw that she still did not comprehend what he was saying. He grabbed her shoulders and said, "Ann, we need to leave. I don't know how to explain it, but we need to get out of here. Please, baby, just help me pack. I have to leave, and you're coming with me."

She resisted at first and tried to pull away from him, but then she looked at the panic embedded into his eyes. "Okay," she said reluctantly. "Where are we going?"

In truth, he didn't know, but he felt something pulling him and seemingly pointing him in the direction he needed to go. "I don't know, baby, but trust me. We need to leave now."

Ann nodded slowly. She knew that she needed to at least humor him. Something had scared him more than anything had before, and she felt it, too—a darkness surrounding them. When they went into the bedroom, she saw how frantically he was packing. She began to feel a sense of dread seize her. It was as though it was a contagion, his panic infecting her, letting his fear seep in and metastasize into something more than she could bear. Her heart was racing, and she frantically searched for anything that she couldn't live without.

They rushed out the door, both dressed too quickly and neither were really aware where they were supposed to go. Scott pulled Ann behind him as she struggled to keep up, her bags weighing more and more with each step as they raced to the street, intent on contacting a cab once they were outside of the encroaching walls. Neither of them spoke on their way to the airport. The cab driver glanced nervously through the rearview mirror several times, trying to make sense of the couple, and when they reached the terminal, he left quickly after receiving a meager tip.

Scott stood patiently in line with Ann, both fidgeting in place, but their nerves had settled considerably once they had left their house. She could now feel the pull inside her, a sense of urgency that propelled them every step of the way. Neither of them discussed it, but when she looked into Scott's eyes, she knew deep down that he felt it as well.

The ticket agent called them up, and she waited patiently as Scott fumbled for his identification. "Destination, sir?" the agent asked.

There was a pregnant pause. Ann hadn't even thought that far ahead. *Where were they going anyway?* She glanced over at Scott, and he smiled as if someone was talking to him. A sense of peace settled onto his face. "Seattle, please. Two one-way tickets."

Chapter 2

There are Always Eyes in the Shadows

> *Only through pain and suffering is the soul purified.*
> *~ Gospel of the Fallen 50:19*

Location: *Vault 665-1, USA.*

Industrial grade air filters sterilized the environment to ensure optimized performance for the user. Within the recesses of Vault 665-1 rested all the intelligence collected within the world. From the technologically advanced nations to those countries still reliant on human asset collection. With a single mouse click its user could secretly start a war or decimate a super power's economy.

This was part of the Assembled's power structure. One of many locations, which allowed them to manipulate the world at a whim. For the organization's second in command today had a more focused agenda. Cincaid had one question, which needed answering. *Was Gabriel Willis dead?* She had lost contact with her Scout. Employing demonic entities could negatively affect satellite communications. It was a regrettable bi-product of their presence, which was another reason she had sent CS to collect a first-hand account of his death.

Accessing the main terminal Cincaid combed through the program. Cross-referencing current assets overhead and other systems she could tap into, she ordered an over flight of the last known area of CS. Cincaid was fluent in multiple languages so she didn't have to wait for the system to translate the authentication prompts. Fluent in

Mandarin, Japanese and Russian, she unlocked the systems rapidly giving her unrestricted access.

The system struggled slightly as it tried to incorporate all the data and accomplish Cincaid's commands. Scouring the dense woods she cycled through multiple image settings. Thermal, infrared, along with several other settings showed her the carnage others would fail to see. CS and her team could be seen slowly moving away, each ensuring their thermal signature looked more like a juvenile bear than a team of highly trained assassins. Residual demonic energies could be seen as incredibly cold thermal imprints upon the ground. Hundreds of signatures were clustered around one specific location. There was a lack of dismembered remains. This fact vexed her. It was possible for the Devourer to engorge itself upon its prey. However this scale of destruction to the vegetation suggested more of a frustration than an animalistic feeding frenzy. Her instincts suggested something had gone wrong, but she would have to wait until CS delivered her report.

Turning from the computer monitor, she cued up the video conferencing screen. Ensuring one-way video was established, she placed a call to the Deputy Director of Red Horse. The clandestine Department of Defense asset could orchestrate the continued monitoring of the area she had just inspected. Commander Miller answered the call immediately. The submissive demeanor of the Active Duty Navy Commander told Cincaid his loyalties were still to her organization. It was a considerable long shot placing any overhead assets in the area to find Mr. Willis. Historical documents retained in the Assembled's archives were vague on details pertaining to the gifts reserved for the Saints. No one knew if it was riches, artifacts, or something with unimaginable power. The only thing they knew for sure was the enemy wanted it badly, so she needed to take it away. Drones could accomplish the task; truthfully she didn't care how the area was monitored, just so long as any changes could be acted upon immediately. Her voice was smooth as she addressed the Naval Officer. "Commander Miller, I am in need of the services your organization can provide. In the encrypted file I just sent you is a location I want monitored. I am looking for anything out of the ordinary."

He nodded and looked off screen for a moment before returning his attention to the blank monitor. "Mistress I will accomplish your order without fail. There seems to be a geographic correlation between your request and an event we are tracking. May I pass along this recent development, which I was going to route through the normal channels. The details are still in the infancy stage, however I can keep you abreast on them as well."

After giving her consent Miller continued, "Within the last few hours we have seen an alarming increase in ticket sales to Washington State. Our data centers are scrubbing the new passenger lists to see if there is any correlation between them, and at the moment it all seems to be a strange coincidence. Your request being in the same state leads me to think there may be more to this than I am privy to understand."

She considered the possibilities for a minute and then issued her guidance, "Keep me posted on the numbers and if any of these new travelers seem to be going toward the location I sent you."

"As you desire Mistre..."

She cut the link before Commander Miller could finish his sentence. This was an interesting turn of events. There was a multitude of reasons for the influx of travelers, however the one that plagued her the most was the idea that they were coming to find Gabriel Willis.

The constant buzz in her pocket pulled her away from the monitor. Two lines of a text message appeared on her phone, and she was moving toward the exit before she finished reading the first one. *Condition critical, all local assets required. Faith seal has been breached, the innocents are being slaughtered.*

Chapter 3

You Never Plan to Fail—You Only Fail to Plan

You will need to answer the questions in their hearts and minds.
~ Semyaza, Commander of the Twelfth Legion

Location: Chicago, Illinois, USA

Within the confines of the armored vehicle there was an air of over-opulence. Tinted, bulletproof glass concealed a state of the art interior, complete with encrypted digital access as well as creature comforts only available to the social elite. Externally the vehicle appeared to be an enlarged, early model of the Chevy Suburban. Chipped paint and other superficial body damage allowed it to blend into the urban streets of Chicago. As with any metropolitan area, the city was broken into different districts. For Cincaid's purposes they were in the most impoverished. She paid no attention to the crumbling structures surrounding her, instead she scrolled through reports on her tablet detailing the situation at their destination.

The text message had come from the confidential account of the Archdiocese of Chicago. There was an axiom she had overheard when she was a child; "the devil is in church every Sunday." Her lord Uther believed that not only was the manipulation of the world's governments essential; but humanities faith networks as well. The upper echelons of the *church* operated in a fractured state to allow maximum reach. This allowed her altered identity with the clergy to be established with the simplistic generation of false documents and then a commitment of time to interact with all the key players. Once the façade had taken, it required the smallest maintenance.

A small group of nuns were gaining influence among the leadership within Rome. While considered on the outside of the traditional organization, their council and help was often solicited by ranking members of the clergy. Cincaid's persona of Mother Genti was among their most well-known, yet rarely seen, members of the group.

Her attention was pulled from the reports when her driver spoke, "Mistress we have arrived at site 931."

Stopping the SUV in the center of a failed social project of the 1930's, the *Commons* was intended to be an urban utopia. A solid iron portrait of its original design was affixed to a pedestal in an overgrown garden, showing its intended purpose of being a place where work and play could be harmoniously intertwined. Seen as a way to lift the city out of the grips of the great depression, the grand aspirations began to fall apart upon its completion. Finished as WWII was beginning, those originally chosen to occupy the housing were shipped off to Europe and ruin and misfortune seemed to plague the Commons ever since.

In its current state, the once impressive seven building complex was an affordable housing project. Dressed in a nun habit, Cincaid exited the SUV and noticed the odd absence of noise, with 1,192 residents, there was typically something going on. A scream pierced the oppressive feeling beginning to build, bringing a cruel smile to her lips. *It seems the residents of the Commons are obeying their fear instinct, that will make things easier,* she thought to herself.

Motioning for the driver to follow her into the center building, the sound of muffled screams coursed through the courtyard area, as the pair moved inside. As the structures seven stories loomed overhead there was nothing left of the hope which once resided here. The residents were isolationists. They preferred to remain ignorant to the fate of their neighbors, and even the presence of two teams of catholic priests caused confusion when it came to seeking help.

Crossing the open-air atrium, Cincaid's lips curled in a sinister grin. The pleading voices rained down from the floors above. Bypassing the inoperable elevator, she took the stairs. Off-white, cinderblock walls stood sentry as she ascended to the fifth floor. Cresting the stairs she could see her destination. A small group of clergy gathered together administering first aid and comforting one another. The room they huddled outside of was the focal point of the vocalized torment. As she exited the stairwell one of the sisters, flushing a deep cut upon the cheek of a priest, caught sight of her and raced toward her. Short of breath she greeted her superior, "Mother Superior, our efforts are falling short. We need more help, Father Mica..." before she could finish the sentence a thunderous impact struck the closed door of the apartment.

Startled cries erupted from the huddled mass. As she moved closer to the apartment door she could hear a female voice shouting profanities toward heaven for an instant before a silence fell upon them. Sensing the narrow window of opportunity Cincaid walked into the room before any objections could be uttered.

Moving slowly, deeper into the apartment her scapular grew stiff and began to crust over with ice. Her religious garments were only for show, so her hand closed around the only source of spiritual power she had brought with her into the room; a small medallion which she wore around her neck. She could feel the otherworldly power coursing through the air. The Smith and Wesson 9mm in the small of her back was useless in this setting, only the charm from Ancient Greece could aid her here. This was why she had come. With the loss of the gathering house in Port Angeles, the need for another nexus point where they could re-establish their connection with the dark planes was critical.

Clearly the involvement of the clergy was antagonizing the corrupt entities, which were invading just below the surface in the Commons. Social injustices, destitute living conditions, and a self-indulgent attitude provided the perfect conduit for the manifestation of malicious spirits. It was a delicate dance, once a breach was found, the demonic presence needed to be enticed, not only to stay, but to call other foul entities forward. This would not only cause untold suffering, but present the ability to gain the insightful knowledge from the damned during their short stay on this plane of existence. With the correct conditions the Commons could provide triple the sacrificial souls as their last location. She cautioned herself, *one step at a time*.

Deep guttural growls came from the back of the apartment. A make-shift collection of construction lighting equipment encircled a small group of men clad in dark, priestly habits. Members of the Roman Catholic Church and Jesuit orders were huddled around a young girl secured to a metal bed frame. Restraints were affixed to her arms and legs causing her to struggle against them as she snarled at each of them through matted hair. The four restraints were affixed to the inter-cardinal directions, keeping the girl in a spread eagle pose. It was a technique used to ensure the victim of possession could not generate any leverage on the restraints and break free. That was all about to change.

"Father Mica?" Cincaid's voice cut though the tension in the air. Women were not allowed in certain venues within the church—exorcism being one of them. However desperate times usually saw the more elitist, dogmatic rules cast aside for the common good. Cincaid had infiltrated the clerical hierarchy for such occasions. Her false document had given her entry, but this was not something she could manifest on paper. It had taken time to nurture the relationships, to establish her worth. She knew Father Mica well. They had worked several possession cases in the past. Now they interacted sparsely. Counterfeit orders from Rome kept her on special assignment. In her earlier days working with Father Mica, he had benefited from her drive and unique understanding of demonic entities and through this relationship they had risen through the ranks quickly. Cincaid felt the church was undeserving of her talents, but her master had been pleased when she had informed him of how deeply she had penetrated their hierarchy.

The collective group looked her way as Father Mica spoke, "Reverend Mother Genti, it is good to see you. I fear Rome is still unable to send us adequate aid. They say there are simply too many cases in need of validation before the few ordained exorcists can be deployed. In their words, we are on our own."

The look of determination set upon the collection of priests, forced Cincaid to suppress a wicked grin. These fools were being manipulated by forces beyond their comprehension. Without further discussion the group of exhausted faith peddlers refocused on their task. Cincaid took up a customary position upon the outskirts of their circle. Her senses dismissed the terrible condition of the living room. All the furniture had been pushed to the sides. At its center was the metal bed frame with the small girl secured via rusty chains and duct tape around her frail limbs. The lack of formality would have vexed a true member of the church's elite. But Cincaid saw only opportunity in every ill executed religious rite. The small girl was still for the moment, however Cincaid knew that would change rapidly. It was ironic how the Papal Seat of Rome continued to exclaim their authority over the ethereal when the collective body of the church didn't have any notion of what the soul truly was; or how to protect it.

Father Mica began to recite the Lord's Prayer while casting holy water onto the ravaged girl. The blessed liquid hissed and burned as it came into contact with exposed skin. The victim of possession still struggled to reach the gathering of clergy. The group encircled the bed frame and all began to echo Father Mica's prayer. At the conclusion of the third iteration tremors began to course through the possessed body. Cincaid noticed the visible drop in room temperature as visible streams of breath began to cloud before their faces.

Thrashing and animalistic barks erupted from the thin lips of the girl. A choir of different vocal patterns all seemed to scream at once. Blood began to puddle upon the ground as she pulled against the restraints. Lacerations appeared at the girl's wrists, and up her arms from an invisible assailant as each word of the prayer was recited. Father Mica looked at Cincaid, "Mother Superior would you lead us in the expulsion rite?" Exhausted from the two-day battle with evil, the priests looked to her for energy. She nodded and moved forward joining the circle.

The possessed girl turned her head to regard Cincaid. A wicked smirk crept across her face. She spoke through shattered teeth and an endless stream of bloody saliva, which flowed, out of her mouth. "It has been many years since that mark has been worn on this plane of existence." The possessed girl was referring to the Greek medallion Cincaid wore under her habit. Her voice was deeper and older than any she could have made on her own. "The whispers in the ether are true then. They are gathering..." A sickly, wet laugh filled the room as Cincaid moved closer to the demonic presence.

Cincaid's voice was forceful and clear as she addressed the being, this development was more intriguing than a simple corruption of a soul. There were potential secrets to be learned from this entity. "This is an old trick, foul one. The wicked often seduce with unknowable information. Who is gathering?" The sadistic smile remained fixed upon the girl's face as Cincaid pulled out a black marker from the depths of her habit. With her cohorts looking on, she moved to the side of the bed and tore open the girls pants to expose her bare leg. The demonic entity began to thrash and bark savagely knowing something was going to happen.

"Mother Superior?" Father Mica's question was met with a gesture for him to remain silent.

"The damned are both tricksters and truth sayers. As we become exposed to their lies and secrets we must determine the validity of any statement because it may be a critical nuance the church may have overlooked." Before she could be interrupted she continued, while simultaneously drawing ruinistic shapes onto the girls bare flesh. "My question, foul one, is who is gathering?"

The barrage of animal barks continued as Cincaid finished drawing on the girl's exposed leg. She leaned over to look directly into the eyes of the possessed girl. "I know you can feel it. The runes will compel you to answer my questions. Do I need to continue taking such drastic action?" She could see the fear building in the small girl's eyes. It was primal, instinctive and justified. Before her arrival into the room the demonic presence had been the dominant predator. It was realizing that was no longer the case.

In a universe of unimaginable possibilities, knowledge was coveted power. Whether it was in the form of forgotten capabilities of the human mind, or a location holding untold treasure thought lost for eternity. Whoever possessed creation's secrets would shape the world to come. This was one of the benefits of the gathering houses. The amplification of human suffering aided in the next step to serve the true power within creation. Pain on such a large scale could be channeled on both the planes of hell and humanities reality. Through years of studying the dark arts, Uther knew how to harness it, as well as control it.

If she orchestrated this interaction correctly it could benefit her master greatly. A pain laced moan emanated from the girl, quickly followed by a torrent of projectile bloody gore from every orifice. Before Cincaid could speak she felt the firm grip of Father Mica on her arm, "That is enough! Rome may grant you certain latitudes, but they are not here. This ends now!"

Sensing what was to come, the girl began to scream at the top of her lungs, "Kill him! Kill him!"

Father Mica turned to inspect the girl and saw a crazed smile staring back at him. The lead priest of the small team didn't see Cincaid move to his side. His momentary illusion of control shattered along with his knee as she broke it. Before he landed onto the ground crying out in pain, Cincaid was attacking the other priests. Seconds passed as bone and vertebra snapped leaving the team of clergy dead, except Father Mica. Standing over the wounded man, she picked up a broken discarded table leg. Holding it like a bat, she swung at the other knee of Father Mica, shattering it as well. Ignoring his screams of pain, Cincaid stood above the possessed girl, gripping her chin tightly to force the dark entity to make eye contact. "You know a secret I desire. I do not have time for games, so my offer is this. Your freedom, as well as your jailer. His death may be by your hands, if you tell me; who is gathering."

Chunks of tissue and broken teeth dribbled from the girl's mouth. The multitudes of deep voices echoed as it spoke. "A barter unequal in terms, yet can be fulfilled if these eyes may gaze upon the object you wear around your neck."

She pulled the charm out and pinched it between two fingers. A dull ache in her fingers told her the wards were working to keep her safe. She stood her ground and didn't get any closer to the demon.

"Ahhh...the mortal world can craft even the most malefic symbols into a thing of beauty. The end approaches then. For it is said when next that sigil dominates the dammed, then the end is neigh. Your question is simple yet its answer carries implications. Humanity begins its gathering, more specifically, its Saints. For one destined to lead them stands ready."

The answer was not the news she had wanted to hear. There was a possibility that it could be a lie, however in her gut she knew there was truth in the demonic presence's statement. A concussive wail erupted from the girl as the demon raged at not being set free. A pair of gunshots were drowned out by the unnatural volume of the scream. It looked expectantly at Cincaid, "The other restraints?"

She shook her head as she watched Father Mica attempt to pull himself toward the door. "You can free yourself by your own means; this will make the hunt more enjoyable for you."

Turning to leave she heard the girls fists slamming into her ribs, shattering several. With her torso fractured she was able to get her teeth onto her knees. Tearing the flesh from her finger tips the girls worked frantically to claw and tear at her knee joints, intent on separating herself from the still secured lower half of her legs.

Moving toward the door Cincaid could hear Father Mica's weak pleas for help over the demon's frantic tearing of flesh. He was close to blacking out from shock. Cincaid paused at the exit to the apartment and waited until the priest's weak calls for help changed to frantic wails of torment. The possessed girl finally freeing herself, now fed upon the last clergy member in the room. "Enjoy his flesh ancient one." She said over her shoulder, "Remember this agreement in the future when I call into the darkness. Should you answer, I can provide even more supple flesh to taste."

Gathering herself, she paused and then flung open the door and rapidly exited the apartment, slamming it behind her. Dawning a fictitious look of horror and breathing rapidly, she clung to the nearest clergy member. There was never any question about what transpired in the room. Through manufactured hysteria she told them of how the priests had died. Father Mica had died to save her. Some had tried to go in, but she had held them at bay under the guise of utter fear. In truth, the possessed girl would die in a matter of minutes; consuming flesh until her stomach would burst. While sepsis would have killed her, the indescribable pain would be the final blow. Cincaid had seen this play out many times before.

After five minutes she collected herself and tried to join another exorcism team. As she planned, the priests and nuns had insisted she go back to the Diesis to recover. They would send word when they needed more help. With the ruse complete, she exited the Commons. As she settled into the armored SUV her cell phone chimed. The message was brief, and she ordered her driver to take her to the private airstrip on the outskirts of the city. Her Lord wanted to relocate, and as with all things—his will be done.

Chapter 4

Evil has Many Names—Those That Serve It Have but One...Damned

What can tempt the heart of man to stray from the will of his Creator? Lust, power and success are poison fruit offered by the great deceiver.
~ *Gospel of Babel 87:65*

Location: *The Schloss, Germany*

Soft wind glided across the open grassland. The tranquil sounds of fall lingered in the air. A single, black sedan drove smoothly down a cobblestone drive toward a massive *schloss* that sat on the German countryside. The polished car navigated the uneven terrain with ease, a true testament to the skillful engineers that had designed the luxury automobile. It came to a stop at the entrance to the schloss, and a stream of people spilled out of the main entrance.

The German castle seemed to tower over the surrounding countryside. Each of the servants, dressed in seventeenth-century clothing, stood rigid in rehearsed positions as the chauffeur stepped from the driver's side and walked around to the far side of the car. A casual observer would have assumed that the entire countryside froze, even the breeze quieted for a moment as the chauffeur pulled open the door and allowed one of the two occupants to step out. Dressed in an immaculate black suit, a man of obvious authority stood for a moment and looked at the impressive stone structure before him.

The staff remained fixed in their place as the suited man waited for the chauffeur to open the door on the other side of the car, allowing Cincaid to exit. She walked over to join Uther, and the two looked at the assembled staff. The head butler, solemn and pressed, walked briskly toward the couple and then said, "My Lord Uther, you have graced us earlier than we anticipated...thank you. All of your requests have been fulfilled, and we humbly await any orders you have." The butler bowed deeply and then backed away to join the ranks of his fellow staffers.

Uther looked them over and nodded in dismissal. Powerful eyes scanned over the assembled group, and let out a long, tired sigh. "You may show us in. There will be no inspection today."

The head butler didn't miss a beat. Tall and lanky, he departed from the line of staff and bowed slightly again, "If you would follow me, Lord Uther and Mistress Cincaid, I will show you to your sanctuary."

Both Uther and Cincaid nodded and fell into step behind the butler. This was one of many strongholds controlled by the powerful group and only accessed by the elite of the Assembled. There was little in the way of disguising the massive amount of wealth that Uther possessed, so he chose to display it openly instead of trying to disguise it, thus defusing the slew of media intent on making a name for themselves.

There was no chance of interruption here at the schloss. Fourteen-foot-tall fences surrounded the one-hundred-acre estate. Hidden within a thick mass of trees, the structure gave the impression that it had simply appeared one day out of nowhere. Razor wire kept the non-persistent onlooker from trespassing, and the buried land mines kept the more determined interlopers at bay. Strategists within the military would be hard-pressed to find a more fortified location, if they knew it existed. For all intents and purposes, this was simply a home away from home for a wealthy government consultant. The fact that the man in question was affiliated with every superpower on the planet was a topic that was never discussed but always understood by the social and political elite.

The sound of Cincaid's cloak sliding across the marble floor reverberated off the beautiful seventeenth-century walls. The butler led the mute pair down a long corridor flanked with beautifully crafted paintings of past owners of the estate. None of them were affiliated with the previous owner, but Uther felt the need to keep the portraits for the purpose of appearances. The trio walked for several minutes, and then the butler stopped at an ornate door. "As instructed, my lord, only key members of the staff on the premises have entered your chambers and prepared them for you. The list you requested is within the center drawer of the desk."

Uther walked past the man, not even acknowledging the fact that he had spoken.

Cincaid stopped and locked eyes with the butler, "Have the lower chambers been prepared as well?"

The butler nodded his head respectfully again. "Here is the list of those individuals, mistress, as you requested. Only the head maid and I performed those preparations. Should you find anything out of place, the blame lies squarely with me. In accordance with your instructions, I did not perform any of the necessary preparations in the master's chambers. I spent all my time in the lower chambers and only entered and exited using the subterranean passageway. Should you need anything—"

Cincaid held up her hand and turned from the man. There was no need for pleasantries as the two departed. Cincaid walked into the large suite, and looked at her master behind the ornately designed wooden desk. He was holding a sturdy piece of parchment that he had pulled from the center drawer in the desk. Thirteen names were scrawled upon the handmade paper, each name carefully created with a quill and ink. Uther examined the paper with piercing eyes and then handed it to Cincaid as she joined him, "That was very ingenious of you to ensure the butler didn't enter my chambers, my dear. I see you are growing tired of training new personnel."

Cincaid was about to comment when Uther raised his hand, stopping her short, "There is no need for conversation. There is much to do. I want a status report from our scout, and you know what to do with the names on the list."

Cincaid studied the list for several seconds and memorized all the names. She looked back up from the parchment, meeting her master's gaze. "Would you like to talk to the scout personally, or would you like me to handle it?"

Uther waved her away, "Your powers of intelligence-gathering will suffice for the simple report. I need to prepare to pass our news to the messenger of the host. The death of Gabriel has become a critical task; however, my attention is needed elsewhere." Uther stood slowly and then continued, "I need time alone, Cincaid. Ensure I have it.

With that, he turned and walked to the back of the room, where a collection of ornate library shelves rested on what appeared to be solid wooden walls. Uther's strong hands gripped one of the corners of the shelving, and he pulled slightly. The unit swiveled on a hinge and opened as smoothly as any door. Without comment or a backward glance, Uther stepped into the shadows and disappeared into the darkness behind the bookshelf.

Cincaid stood silent for a moment with the parchment in her hand. Uther wanted a status report from her agent in the field, their departure from Washington had delayed it. She had not spoken of what the entity had told her in the Commons. There was a need to verify all knowledge obtained through such means.

Her mind revisited the issues systematically, and she pulled the cell phone from her back pocket. Her fingertips danced over the keypad, and she held the phone up to her ear. The solemn sound of a male voice told her she had connected to the number she had dialed, "Authentication code?" Then she typed "5242." There was a rush of static, and the phone clicked. "Mistress, how may I be of assistance?" The smooth voice of the senior acolyte caressed her ear. His abilities with the dark arts made him a powerful tool in the Assembled's arsenal; however, his unique gifts could not be turned off, so those of the Assembled who worked closely with any of the acolytes possessed a stout resolve to resist their charms.

She fought the intoxicating underlying tones and focused her mind to keep everything in perspective. The acolytes possessed a gift of persuasion that was unprecedented in society, and Uther had refined their talents a hundredfold. The simplest suggestive comment could commit countries to war or collapse an economy.

Her voice lowered as she fought for control, "I need a status report from CS and the Devourer." Her mind continued fighting against the preternatural skill of the acolyte. It didn't even register that she had used the nickname for her agent and the common name of the demon that the acolytes had bound for their master's dark purposes. There was a notable sigh on the other end of the phone.

"Mistress, with your rapid departure from the main temple, you missed her report by only thirty minutes. She has departed this location via secure transportation to join you at your current residence and deliver the report in person."

Cincaid began to pace the floor. This was not good news. The report should have been delivered to the acolytes so they could generate the needed incantations for the next wave of rituals. There was a soft knock on the door, which drew Cincaid's attention. "No further information required," she said as she ended the call. Her voice was crisp, her militant personality beginning to take control again. Her hand gripped the large brass handle of the door, and a strange sense of déjà vu came over her.

The moment passed quickly, and she swiftly pulled open the door. The butler stood there. "Mistress, forgive the disturbance, however, a woman has arrived who claims to be a member of your staff. She insists she must talk to you at once. We tried to remove her, however she has rendered seven of my security staff to the dark abyss."

Cincaid knew at once who had arrived. She relished the fact that CS had taken on seven security members. It was a testament to her tutelage and training regimen, but now that she was here, there were more pressing matters to attend to. "Take her to the audience chamber on sublevel two. I will talk to her there. I want you to give her something so she knows what you speak is the truth." Cincaid pulled out the pistol that she kept in the small of her back and pulled the slide back, ejecting one round. The pointed red-tipped bullet was one of Cincaid's personal designs. It had taken four years to develop;

however, the lethality of the round and its nearly flawless ballistic quality had made the endeavor worthwhile. The butler bowed slightly and took the round graciously and then walked briskly back down the corridor.

Cincaid closed the door quietly again and looked back at where her lord had walked into the darkness behind the bookcase. The passage led down into a dark and secluded network of massive caves, each one earmarked for her master's dark dealings. She could feel his presence as if he was right next to her, even though she was positive he was over forty feet below her. For a fraction of a moment, she considered walking down into the darkness and delivering the partial news as well as informing him of the feeling of foreboding concerning their enemy's status, but then thought better of it. The whole picture would be needed, not a partial one.

The sublevels had been what had attracted her master to the schloss's unique design in the first place. The original occupants of the structure, some three thousand years ago, had begun its construction from the caves up. Four stories below the ground floor of the building was the lowest point in the network of enormous caves and interconnecting tunnels, but this was not the truly masterful part. Each level had been carved out beneath the one above. There had not been a single thing actually built, but rather there had been countless decades of work done to hollow out the intricately beautiful structures that now stood the test of time.

Sublevel two was lavishly decorated. Its purpose was to act as the secluded meeting area for all discreet engagements that needed to take place at the sanctuary. There were only a handful of people who knew about the existence of the subterranean levels. All visitors had their suspicions, but strict security protocols ensured anyone conducting formal engagements with key leaders of the Assembled never truly comprehended their exact location.

CS sat motionless on the lavish carpet of one of the waiting areas. Her eyes were shut and her body was in a state of meditation. Cincaid watched the scout's rhythmic breathing on the high-definition monitor at the security station near the entrance point to the level. Its formidable construction was masked by creature comforts and distracting accents. The four security officers who sat inside the fortified structure would simply pull a lever to access four assault rifles, two machine guns, and more ammunition and flash grenades than any of them could carry.

Each of them watched the monitor coldly, and Cincaid could see the palpable anger threatening to overcome their professionalism at the loss of seven of their comrades by this woman, who weighed barely more than one hundred pounds. She didn't fault them for the hatred, and knew it would motivate them to train harder so that perhaps only four of their comrades would die by the hands of her scout next time. Cincaid walked down the corridor. The walls and false ceiling gave the impression they were in a hotel rather than a place that was twenty feet below the earth, encased in solid rock. She paused at the door to collect her thoughts. Good news or bad, she forced her mind to wrap around each possibility, ensuring that she would focus on the next step and not on the impact of the information itself.

CS rose quickly to her feet as Cincaid entered the room. There were no furnishings in the waiting area, and Cincaid stopped several paces from CS and waited for her to speak. CS bowed lavishly and said, "My mistress, I come with distressing news. The Devourer has failed, and while the enemy has suffered casualties, they have sealed the entrance of Ephesus."

Cincaid paused, allowing the information to sink in.

CS extended a small data DC and waited for Cincaid's full attention, "All events were recorded per your usual request. Events transpired rapidly and while I did discharge several rounds at the targets, you can see they only missed by a fraction of an inch—a miss, nonetheless"

The back of Cincaid's hand lashed out, and the power behind the strike sent CS slamming into the wall. They had played this deadly game enough, and CS did nothing to stop the full impact of the blow. Each of them knew that the recording of the meeting would be reviewed at great length by Uther, and if the punishment was not severe enough, he would handle it himself. And that would mean one of Cincaid's most talented agents would be reduced to a lifeless corpse, a sacrifice to the dark beasts lurking in the shadows.

Cincaid's hand flashed out again, this time striking CS square in the nose. The resounding crack hung in the air as Cincaid followed up the strike with her free hand, grabbing CS's hair and yanking down hard. With her neck now exposed, Cincaid's hand shot like a knife, cutting into CS's windpipe. Reflex took over, and the next attack was blocked. Cincaid recovered quickly and looked at her prodigy. Now the dance would truly begin. Cincaid didn't fault CS for not simply taking the beating. It showed how strong-willed she was, and as each of them had discussed in the past, the show would take the pressure off any punishment that might follow the delivery of such terrible news.

They circled the room, each evaluating the other. Cincaid moved in quickly while CS was midstep, her leg swinging wide. CS blocked the attack easily, but left her midsection open. Cincaid struck with both hands, the force sent CS reeling toward the far wall. Cincaid pressed her attack. Three strikes found their mark, and CS quickly rolled away, her face bloodied. Cincaid lashed out again with her dangerous jab, and CS looped her arm and flung her over her shoulder. Cincaid simply rolled to a squatting position; however, CS pounced before Cincaid could get her bearings. CS slammed her knee into the side of Cincaid's face. The force of the blow blurred Cincaid's vision for a few seconds—seconds that CS used to her advantage.

A barrage of blows fell upon Cincaid, her reflexes deflecting them as she tried to get her bearings. Cincaid rolled under a potentially devastating attack, striking CS's tibial nerve in her right leg. CS's leg failed to respond to her command to turn, and Cincaid attacked in the moment of hesitation. The pair rolled, and Cincaid pinned CS below her. The adrenaline flowing through her body nearly caused her to kill CS out of reflex. Her mind quickly pulled control away from her muscles as her fist slammed painfully into the floor.

Cincaid quickly recovered and gripped the loose collar of CS's shirt. As she crossed her hands and twisted them into the fabric, Cincaid created a nearly flawless choke hold. CS thrashed below her. She only had seconds before her brain would be deprived of enough blood to cause her to black out. Those precious seconds passed too quickly, as CS's eyes soon rolled up in her head and the taut body that had once thrashed below Cincaid went limp. Cincaid continued the beatings for another two minutes, ensuring to avoid lethal areas. Then she simply stopped, picked up the data disk and the bullet she had passed to CS from the floor, straightened herself up, and walked out the door. Her footsteps were crisp, and as she came upon the security station, the smug looks vanished from the guards' faces as they met her eyes. "Summon the medical staff and ensure her injuries are treated. Should any harm befall this agent, your lives will be forfeit. Do I make myself clear?" All four of the men stood and nodded. She could hear their frantic voices on the phone as she continued down the stone steps leading to the level below.

Cincaid flexed her hands as she made her way down to her master's subterranean chamber. Necessary evils were a daily occurrence for her, but seeing CS bloodied on the floor pulled at the small tendrils of humanity that were buried deep within her. Her master was her world but CS was her guilty pleasure. Everything she had deprived herself was neatly packaged in CS. Forbidden love, mentorship, trust, and even some twisted malformed maternal bond. A warm glow flared inside Cincaid as she mentally saw CS's recovery; necessary evils to influence the future to suit her needs.

Even with the injuries to CS fading from her mind, Cincaid felt an oppressive weight begin to push down on her shoulders as she descended to the lower levels. Nothing had surprised her since their first arrival to the European sanctuary three years before. She had been witness to no less than twenty rituals designed to change the very fabric of the subterranean structure into something much more sinister. And she could feel the changes beginning to take effect now. It had been subtle at first, but now the malevolence of the soil and rock that surrounded her was running like a raging torrent.

Lost in thought, she descended to the lowest level. She stopped in front of her private chamber door, and slipped quietly inside and over to the desk at the far side of the sparsely decorated room. There was a simple bed, office furniture, and an area to pray—not in the way that many other people thought of the act, but a lone place where she could mentally rehearse the dark rituals her master required. There was a black laptop on the desk, and she inserted the data CD. The computer hummed to life, and the images began to play across the screen. The vantage point was pristine, and Cincaid could see the small outcropping in the center of the picture.

A set of stones covered in vegetation sat surrounded by trees. Her blood began to pump faster as she saw the familiar face of her enemy cross in front of the targeting scope of her scout. Events seemed to play out exactly as she had imagined them during CS's brief description. She watched as the two police officers to whom she had provided information stumbled into the clearing. Their involvement had been activated when she posed as a federal agent to add more assets to kill or capture Gabriel Willis. As the sky darkened on the screen, Cincaid could see the realization dawn on the small group, their faces shifting from confusion to fear.

The image shifted, and Cincaid knew CS was moving into position for a kill shot. The image righted itself again, and the crosshairs rested on Gabriel's chest. A flash of movement caught Cincaid's eye as something moved in front of CS's target. She stopped the recording and slowly rewound the video file. She froze the image and enlarged it. Cincaid knew immediately who it was. The glowing symbol she had seen on the back of the woman's neck was one Cincaid herself had carved. Gabriel's wife was going into the temple, and if Cincaid was correct, the acolytes were just about to trigger her.

CS saw the blurred image and was distracted for the briefest instant. This was all it took. Chaos erupted at the site, and CS fired two shots as Gabriel pulled both police officers into the hole. Cincaid could trace the trajectory of both silenced shots and saw that CS had missed her target by only a fraction of an inch. It wouldn't matter to Uther. The mistake had allowed his prey to elude him again, and there would be consequences for failure. Her mind went back to the image of the symbol on Jennifer's neck. Her hand grabbed the phone again, and she quickly hit redial.

Chapter 5

There is Never Any Time for Reflection

In fact, everyone who wants to live a godly life in Christ will be persecuted, while evil men and impostors will go from bad to worse, deceiving and being deceived.
~ 2 Timothy 12-13

Location: Ephesus

Gabriel sat silently against a dirt wall, his sleeping daughter nestled in his lap. Dirty, worn, and visibly frayed, an ancient parchment he gently gripped in his bloodstained hands held detailed information its reader wouldn't have believed—until a few weeks ago. A soft light cascaded from the ceiling, allowing his gleaming, blue eyes to focus on the ancient drawing.

Gabriel didn't know where the illumination came from; however, he instinctively understood that a sense of awe should be associated with the unknown source of light, which existed throughout the massive subterranean chamber along with each sub-chamber that broke off of the main edifice. But so much had transpired over the course of a few weeks that this small miracle went relatively unnoticed.

Fate, some say, is nonexistent, while others claim that a divine influence shapes and molds our lives. Gabriel could have had a normal life, had a blissful veil of ignorance shielding him not been lifted. That blessing given to all humanity allowed him a peaceful existence, safe from the abominations that lurked in the darkness.

His former life forgotten, his eyes now fully aware of the true horrors that the universe had to offer.

Throughout mankind's reign on the earth, there had been stories of suffering for the greater good, the noble sacrifice made by the few for the protection of the many. Gabriel's mind often pondered those stories and how hollow and unrealistic they would now sound to him. Their heroes always asked to bear unspeakable pain, misery, suffering, and loss so that those who would never know of their existence could live their lives in blissful ignorance. How could those stories ever have a happy ending? How could his? In those stories, humanity's most vulnerable moment required much from those few. Could anyone truly blame them if they faltered in heeding the call? Could anyone blame him if he simply said "no"?

The tattered shell of the formerly peaceful man looked like nothing the powers-that-be had hoped for. Despair was slowly unraveling his mind, the last in a bloodline that reached back thousands of years. If his shattered consciousness would allow his mind to remember his biblical history, he could have drawn parallels between his suffering and that of other key figureheads throughout its divinely inspired pages—Abraham, Moses, Job, and others who had all told their tales of suffering for the masses—however, none of that would have eased the feeling of loss welling up inside him.

The small form resting on his lap stirred slightly and then settled back into the realm of sleep. A soft grin caressed Gabriel's lips, then his mind drifted to unnerving memories of his wife's screams of pain and the images of his son's body resting in a pool of his own blood. Two days had passed since his wife had become possessed by something beyond Gabriel's imagination, her body shifting and changing before him. Her pleading eyes haunted his dreams. Her cries of anguish and loss echoed in his mind every second.

His daughter was all that was left of his immediate family. Her small frame curled up tightly. Grief, shock, and fatigue pushed her mind deep down, keeping her locked up tight until her body and consciousness would awake and deal with the tragic loss. His little Marie was only four-years old. No one should ever go through what they had, but truly, no child should ever be made aware of the darkness that lurks in every shadow. Gabriel's family and the two women they traveled with had arrived at this underground temple after weeks of heartache, terrible loss, and a path of chaos that stretched from the hills of Afghanistan through the cities of Europe, finally coming to the depths of the wilderness on the western shores of North America.

Pins and needles coursed through Gabriel's lower limbs; he held his daughter close and stood on wobbly legs, trying to fend off the effects of lost circulation. His daughter tried to remain attached to him at all times. The sudden and violent change in her life had driven her need to touch him and validate that he had not left as well. Gabriel didn't blame her. He knew deep down that he needed her to latch on to him as well. During the few moments, each day when she would awaken, her eyes would stay glossed over, a far-off look on her face.

The void that his heart held ached and tears began to flow down his face for the hundredth time as he silently prayed for strength. His heavy footsteps carried him out into the main chamber of his new home. Weariness drained his body as he moved toward a room on the far side of the massive area. Three hundred feet away sat a doorway that opened into a chamber housing millions of texts. He had aptly dubbed it the library and his mind recalled the shelves that were carved into the walls or made of petrified wood, holding countless books, parchment scrolls, and stone tablets.

Marie stirred for a moment and readjusted her head on Gabriel's shoulder. Waves of blond hair spilled over his dirty shirt, and he sighed for a moment. He looked into the library. The walls of black rock were almost invisible behind all the artifacts on the shelves.

His eyes took in the grandeur of the room, and for one split second, his grief was dampened slightly with a feeling of awe. Gabriel walked farther into the room and saw a lone individual nearly buried in a mountain of books and parchment scrolls. The woman who methodically combed through the never-ending sea of ancient literature was Othia.

Gabriel couldn't possibly begin to calculate the depth of the information she was going through, but he was sure it would pay off somehow. Othia, who was slender, olive-skinned, and far more intelligent than he could ever dream of becoming, pored over the books as though they held the secrets of the universe. And truth be told, they might. She was an archeologist. His mind lingered on this fact, because there was little else that he knew about his new friend.

The parchment in his hands drew his attention again, and he looked at the endless amount of notes he had scrolled across it. They had all tried to stay very busy, each doing what they were good at. Othia rarely left the library.

The other member of their team, Samantha, caught his eye as she wandered the main chamber and studied all the artwork that adorned the walls and she joined him, quietly watching Othia go through yet another massive tome pulled from the shelf near her. The trio stood silent, both Gabriel and Samantha entranced by the ritual of data collection going on before them. Othia looked up after a moment and locked eyes with Gabriel. After the weeks they had known each other, Gabriel knew that look all too well. He was about to say something when Othia turned her attention to Samantha. "Well, how are the two of you getting along?" Othia didn't wait for an answer but walked over and joined them. She regarded Marie's slumbering form for a moment and then nodded.

"Gabriel, we need to talk for a second. Do you think Samantha can watch Marie while she is still sleeping?"

Gabriel was about to politely object; however, Othia's expression changed, and he nodded. Gabriel and Samantha contorted their bodies to try to pass the sleeping Marie from one shoulder to another in a vertical game of Twister. It only took a few moments, and then Marie was using Samantha's shoulder as a pillow.

Othia smiled at Samantha. "We'll be back soon." Samantha nodded and began to walk slowly through the rows of books, gently swaying to try to keep the four-year old from waking.

Once Gabriel and Othia exited the library, she looked at Gabriel again. "I think we have a problem."

Gabriel wanted to laugh. No shit they had a problem. Their lives were simply one problem after another. But he held the comment back and waited for Othia to state her case.

"The text I was just examining tells of the construction of the crossbows that we found in the passageway that brought us to this central chamber. I stumbled onto it when I was trying to cross-reference the locations of the different sites like this." Gabriel's face perked up, but she held up her hand. "One issue at a time. This needs our attention first. Look here at the blueprint for the design of the weapon." She pulled out an ancient parchment from her cargo pocket before she continued, "The bolt is where we need to really focus. It says that they were all treated with a kind of serum to infect the damned so that even if they were only wounded, they would perish soon after the battle. It talks about another addition that later artisans made to the weapon. They placed an aggressive pathogen into the wood so that when it came in contact with the human bloodstream, it would spread and kill any human soldiers loyal to the fallen in a matter of days…if they survived the initial battle. Gabriel, I think that Samantha may have infected Detective James with this, and I didn't heal him enough to truly kill this kind of virus."

Gabriel thought of the overweight cop who had showed up right before they had entered the antechamber of this immense temple. He had killed Gabriel's wife, or rather he had killed the demon possessing her, and then turned his gun on them in fear. It was Samantha's quick thinking that had saved them, but now that act might kill them all.

Othia watched Gabriel turn pale as the full weight of this information and its ramifications set in. "Can it spread?"

"I don't know, but we need to go see. I can heal him if he is still alive. There is a passage that talks of accidental exposure and how to treat it, but if he is already dead, we need to get him buried or burned or something…fast."

His mind began to work. He considered different ways to ultimately keep his daughter safe. The frantic thoughts for her safety took over his mind. The mental image of the parchment he had been sketching came to mind. Only one room that he had checked so far was truly isolated. "Okay, let's have Samantha and Marie wait this out in the dark room. Seal it and then get them afterward. Semyaza said God can't see in there. Let's hope that means the virus can't get in there as well."

Chapter 6

No Good Deed Goes Unpunished

It is not surprising, then, if his servants masquerade as servants of righteousness. Their end will be what their actions deserve.
~ 2 Corinthians 11:15

Location: *Ephesus*

The two met outside the chamber door, where Gabriel had placed James days earlier. He had checked on him every few hours; however, James had turned over at the very beginning, and all Gabriel wanted to see was that James was still breathing. He was mentally berating himself when Othia's grip pulled him back to reality. "Marie safe and sound?" Othia asked, and he nodded. "Good. We need to go in now. Ready?"

She didn't wait for his response. She threw open the door. Gabriel relaxed a fraction of a second as he saw James's body slumped in the same fashion that he had seen each time he had looked in on the shackled man.

Othia quietly walked over to his side and looked over James's shoulder. The smell of human waste and rancid body odor assaulted the pair, but neither complained. Gabriel's heart rose to his throat as he watched Othia place her hand over her mouth to keep the bile rising in her throat from spilling onto the floor. He joined her, and he placed his hand on James's shoulder to try to roll him over onto his back. A burning sensation consumed the palm of his hand, and he pulled back quickly. Gabriel glanced down at his palm and noted that it was bright red, inflamed from the contact with James's shoulder. A haggard breath filled the small chamber.

Gabriel looked over James's shoulder and saw what had made Othia's stomach turn. James's skin looked glossy, and it had turned to a dark shade of blue. His veins looked as though they were about to rip right out of his skin. Gabriel looked closer and saw movement in the veins as the blood pumped through them with each beat of James's raging heart. Gabriel looked back at Othia, who was now standing near the doorway, taking in some air.

"Can you heal him? If you can, we need to do it quick. It looks like he is boiling in his own skin."

"It is worse than that. The infection is spreading to his brain and other vital organs. I don't know how this will turn out, but Gabriel, when we tried to heal you, there was a chance that you could turn into..." Othia's voice trailed off as she remembered the fight she and Samantha had waged to free Gabriel from a demon that had manifested inside him. Gabriel shook his head.

"I remember what you said about the slab. Don't worry. If he changes, I will take care of things." To solidify his point, Gabriel unsheathed the sword he carried on his back. Flames surged across the blade as he held it close to James, "Othia, we need to do this now."

She nodded and knelt next to the ailing police detective. She could feel the heat radiating off his body, and she caught another lingering scent of James's decaying flesh.

Othia began to pray, and Gabriel watched her hands jump to life, a pure white flame dancing around her nimble fingers. Gabriel stiffened as James's body began to shake, and he pulled his sword to the ready position, his eyes searching for the faintest threat to Othia. It lasted nearly twenty minutes. The strong rhythmic prayer was powerful, and with each passing second, James's body seemed to be responding favorably. Othia stopped abruptly and turned from James. Her mouth spewed forth a black and gray sludge that splattered onto the wall. She heaved the contents of her stomach several times. Each time, more and more sludge covered the floor near the two of them. Gabriel tried to go to Othia each time, but she held up a hand between the violent outbursts of fluid from her body.

After what seemed an eternity, she looked up at Gabriel and wiped her mouth. "It's done. We need to move him closer to us so I can keep an eye on his recovery."

Gabriel nodded and looked down at James. His color was returning to normal, and his breathing was slow and steady. Gabriel couldn't say for certain, but it looked as though a faint smile was crossing the detective's lips.

"How long do you think he'll be out?"

They both struggled with James's limp form as they carried him into the library. Othia shook her head. "I don't know, but if I'm in here with him, I think I can keep him occupied for a few seconds if he is unruly." Gabriel nodded as he saw her incline her head toward the shotgun resting on one of the tables. They placed James's unconscious form on the ground, and Gabriel re-secured the handcuffs to one of the large table legs.

Gabriel stood and let his eyes wander around the center of the library. The strangeness of handcuffing someone to a table that held thousands of years' worth of information gave him a moment of pause. Then he pushed the thought to the back of his mind. This was truly one of the easy adjustments, considering the endless list of life-changing events that had occurred.

He turned around when he felt Othia's hand on his shoulder, "I need to show you something. It's by the entrance, but at an angle so that if you were not looking, you wouldn't even know it was there."

Gabriel followed her toward the entrance of the chamber, and he paused when his eyes fell upon a massive map tucked to the right of the doorway. Othia was right. It was shadowed, and the architect seemed to want to keep it hidden even by displaying it out in the open. "What is it? Besides the obvious."

"Your soon-to-be empire, for lack of a better word. It is an ancient map of the world, but the geography is essentially the same.

These raised symbols with the writing next to them are temples like this one here." Gabriel watched as Othia ran her fingers down the side of the map; the strange swirling language changed into readable text as he focused, *The strongholds of the saints shall remain untainted by the hands of the fallen.*

Gabriel paused for a moment, trying to remember anything he could about the massive amount of information he had been trying to process for the last several days. Each of them had been trying to sort out the basic facts from the mountains of information in the library. Othia had digested more than Samantha and Gabriel combined, however they all wanted to gain insight into the new direction their lives were going. They wanted a core of understanding so that they all could speak intelligently when others arrived. The vast amount of information left each of them simply wondering where to start, "I assume this is about the one hundred and forty-four thousand saints, right?"

Othia nodded and said, "I think this is the breakdown of your infrastructure, the sites where we can mass forces without the suspicions of local governments making our task even harder. We might stay off the radar for a short while, but I'd wager the people after us have satellites and everything else combing the surface right now."

Gabriel was quiet as he took in this new information, "If this is the support structure, then the number must be accurate. There are seven temples here."

"That's right. They match the churches that John wrote about in the Bible, the Book of Revelation. Scholars have debated what the churches really meant. Some said they were actual churches. Others mentioned that they were a type of code for early followers in Christianity and that the code words were used to allow the documents to remain in the open. But I guess we now know the truth. He was writing to the commanders of these temples, telling them what was to come, how the end was to unfold."

Gabriel nodded his head, "My math isn't what it used to be, but that would mean about twenty-thousand at each site, give or take a few thousand here and there. If this place is any indication of how sparse the living conditions are going to be, then we have our work cut out for us."

Othia looked off in the distance and nodded, "How many days left until they begin to arrive?" she whispered. The guesswork for who would be arriving had been taken out of the equation when the heavenly visitors told both Gabriel and Othia that they would be establishing an army.

Gabriel stopped himself and nearly scoffed at his own generalization of the angels. They weren't polite, dainty, winged visitors. They were imposing mythical beings covered in medieval armor, who forced them to comply with what they claimed was God's will at the time. Gabriel and Othia did not deny what their angelic messengers had told them was the truth. So much had happened to each of them that their faith was no longer in question, just their obedience. For Gabriel that level of blind allegiance was becoming harder to maintain with each passing day.

"Nine days. Will you be ready?"

Othia laughed and spread her arms wide at the contents of the library. "Look at this place. There is no way that I can digest all this in nine days and be some sort of spiritual leader to all the people who are coming. You think the logistics are making your head spin? Try writing something that one hundred and forty-four thousand people are going to follow as if it came from the burning bush."

Chapter 7
Everyone has a Purpose—For Some, it is Dual-Fold

It is striving against that which is perceived as wrong that makes a good leader.
~ Ancient XIII Legion proverb

Location: *Ephesus*

Gabriel's head swam. The mountain of documents resting in front of him was daunting, and every time he made it through one of the massive texts, there were fifty to a hundred left on the table that dealt with the same subject matter. The task had been enlightening, and he would never claim that he hadn't learned invaluable information through the course of his study, but now his brain was on overload. The information was beginning to blend together, and he was struggling to keep it all separated by categories.

His head fell into his hands, and he sat quietly for a moment, simply focusing on his breathing, when a small force slammed into his leg and latched on. His eyes flew open and he looked down. There staring up at him were two beautiful blue orbs of pure brilliance. Puffiness around those stunning eyes caused him to pull her close. "What's wrong?" Eyes filled with a mixture of terror and love stared up at him. He pushed back from the table and pulled his daughter off his leg and hugged her close, smothering her with loving kisses. Marie began to playfully fight off each one, and her delightful laughter warmed his soul.

Gabriel's heart was still a destroyed shell. He knew it would take every ounce of strength to make it until tomorrow, but there was also the need to keep Marie safe. His mind and heart fought for control as his grief began to take hold of his thoughts. They had been through so much in such a short time. He knew she deserved more than this in life, and as the warmth of her unconditional love radiated from her hug, it nearly caused him to spiral down into an abyss of despair.

Samantha hesitated before entering the room, "Sorry, Gabriel, but I figured it was better to have her find you than risk her having a panic attack." Gabriel nodded between playful kisses with his daughter. All three of them agreed that it was very important to keep things upbeat, not only for Marie but for their own mental health as well. Each of them knew the day would come when she would ask the hard questions: *Where did Mommy and Peter go? Why did God make them leave?* A consensus was reached that the truth, without all the gory details, was important and that when that day came, they would try to answer the questions together.

Gabriel let Marie catch her breath, and he smiled affectionately. "Let's take a walk. I could use a break." She jumped down and instantly took Gabriel's hand. It reminded him of their walks around their old neighborhood. It was their private time together. Jennifer and Peter would stay at the house so the one-on-one time could be productive. The memory brought back a flood of emotions, and Gabriel turned his head away to compose himself, but not for the sake of vanity. Samantha and Othia had seen him at his lowest—he wanted to keep Marie's spirits up.

They walked in silence, Marie was enjoying the change of scenery. Samantha cleared her throat and smiled at Gabriel before she asked, "So where are we going?"

Gabriel forced a smile as well, "Let's try going to the well. I think Othia is the only one who has seen it. She says it's breathtaking. She still sleeping?"

Samantha nodded. She had checked on her briefly when Marie had begun to stir. "Sounds great," she said.

The walk would be a pleasant change of pace. Othia had found the chamber called "the well" two days before and had been unable to do it justice with her description—or so she said. She had brought back some refreshing water and a strange ruby-red fruit. Gabriel tried it first, ensuring to take small bites in case it proved poisonous to people. He found it quite delicious and filling, with a strange, light, refreshing quality. Visiting the place had seemed like a completely elective trip, because there was so much to do still, so he had put off going to see it personally.

There had been other chambers that had captivated him, and during their individual investigations, Gabriel had found a chamber filled with unfathomable riches. Samantha had been with Marie when he had found it, so he had only shown it to Othia. The cavernous chamber was close to bursting with priceless treasures of antiquity. Othia speculated that in the chamber rested more wealth than some countries possessed today. Someone had collected it throughout the ages, and here it sat, waiting for them to use it for a higher purpose. It had been a staggering find, but Othia had impressed upon him that the well had been even more wondrous.

Samantha was uncharacteristically quiet next to him, and Gabriel knew she was thinking about asking him something. That was the only time she was quiet. He looked at her and saw her mind searching for just the right way to pitch whatever she was contemplating. "Just ask...or say it already," he finally said.

Samantha looked surprised and then laughed uncomfortably, "That obvious, huh?" Gabriel nodded, and Samantha shrugged. "I think we might need to get a look at what is going on up there." She pointed toward the ceiling, but Gabriel knew she meant outside the temple. "You and Othia have families. You should at least call your folks and tell them you're alive." Gabriel was about to object when

Samantha started talking again. "I don't mean tell them everything, but at least that you are alive and what the news is saying is false. You said everyone thinks you're a terrorist, right? Plus, we need supplies. I didn't plan on living underground the rest of my life when I traveled light for this trip. And to be perfectly frank, you are starting to look like a dirty mountain man, so I must look just as bad."

The lighthearted jab brought about a forced chuckle, and Gabriel's own laughter startled him. For three days straight, he had grieved, and he couldn't remember the last time he had truly laughed. "You're right," he said. Gabriel's mind flashed back to the final meeting he had had with one of Heaven's most powerful warriors. The imposing, armored warrior had arrived after Gabriel and the small group had made their way into the temple. Tempers had flared and the only thing Gabriel knew for sure was that someone was coming in ten days. He didn't know how many people or how they were getting here, but he had the sneaking suspicion his actions may have eliminated the only help he was going to get until he could truly influence things the way he wanted. Samantha was right, of course. There were things he needed to take care of, and this was going to be a significant logistical effort if their army was supposed to total over 140,000 people.

They all continued onward through the gently sloping tunnel. None of them uttered a single word as they rounded the final corner. The mouth of the passageway opened up into an underground orchard. Gabriel's eyes scanned the width of the vast chamber and settled on three trees standing inside a circle of inviting grass. On the trees grew the strange fruit that Othia had brought up to them days earlier. To the right of the small grouping of trees was an underground river that stretched nearly nine feet across, and even though the water was crystal clear, Gabriel could not guess its depth. On the opposite bank of the river, there was a patch of black dirt and then a small tunnel that led into another uncharted segment of the vast network of tunnels around them.

Gabriel took a tentative step into the chamber, and his mind and body instantly relaxed. He wished with all his heart that Jennifer could have been with him to feel the indiscernible peace that filled him as he stood by the river. Marie pulled at her father's hand, and the three of them made their way to the grouping of trees ahead. His eyes took in the lavish green grass, and instantly, he wanted to just lie down on it. Each blade of grass looked a million times more plush and inviting than any bed he had ever slept on. His body ached to lie down and relax, but his soul warned him that this was not a place for sleep but of rejuvenation. To lie here and waste what little time they had would have bordered on travesty.

Gabriel pulled down three pieces of fruit, and each of them sat against the trunk of the tree. Gabriel instantly relaxed as his back rested against the ancient bark, as he enjoyed the sweet taste of the strange red morsel sliding down his throat. He passed the fruit to the others, and smiled at his daughter's shining face.

"This is a special place, cutie, but you know that already, don't you?"

Marie's head bobbed up and down as she stuffed as much of the fruit into her mouth as possible. Gabriel eased close to her, and she leaned against him. The trio sat quietly for several moments.

Gabriel looked at Samantha. She was enjoying things as much as he was. "Thank you for the break," he said. "I needed it. You're a good friend. I know things are going to get crazy in the near future, and we are all going to be caught up in the excitement, so I wanted to thank you for everything in advance. All of us have been through a lot, and I can only guess that the worst is yet to come. But I feel truly blessed that we are all together."

Samantha sat speechless for several seconds, then smiled sheepishly at Gabriel. Her voice was quiet when she responded, "Do you remember when I asked for you to please let me stay with you and Othia when we were in Europe?"

Gabriel had nearly forgotten the conversation. It seemed like a lifetime ago, but it had really only been a few weeks. Othia and Gabriel had tried to go on alone after the police became involved when they escaped the enemy. That notion had been a misplaced sense of chivalry, one that Gabriel now saw.

He nodded and said, "I remember."

"That day, I considered you all my family, and I can't tell you how happy I am that we are together. It's hard to explain, Gabriel, but now I finally feel as though I belong somewhere. Does that sound strange?"

Gabriel leaned back and took another bite of the fruit. His arm rested around Marie, and his ears registered the crunch of her tiny teeth tearing into her food. "Not at all, Samantha. This place is truly a gift. In fact, I would be almost optimistic about our chances, except for seeing firsthand how fast things can change."

Gabriel looked down, and his heart was thankful that Marie had not caught on to the comment. Her eyes distant, Samantha nodded as she recalled the violent passing of Gabriel's wife and son. She cleared her throat, her emotions trying to get the better of her. "We will all get through this together. Whatever you need, both Othia and I are here for you. You know that, right?"

Gabriel nodded and smiled.

Chapter 8

The Questions Will Need an Answer

Fear the Lord, you his saints, for those who fear him lack nothing.
~ Psalm 34:9

Location: *Ephesus*

Time passed, and Gabriel felt the information begin to take root, building up his confidence. The message from the angel named Semyaza rang in his mind: "Soon, the saints will begin to arrive." There was little else to do, and with only two days remaining until the first wave of people arrived, Gabriel was nearly ready. Both he and Othia had been given a vast amount of knowledge from their angelic messengers; however, the information seemed fleeting until it was triggered by some fact that allowed their minds to grasp the true meaning of the data.

Samantha walked into the library. Even disheveled, she still had a vibrant spark that radiated in her eyes. She looked fondly at Othia and Gabriel hunched among hundreds of books, their intent faces locked in concentration on whatever facet of ancient history they were studying. Gabriel looked up and smiled. Before he could say anything, Samantha nodded and said, "She's sleeping right outside. My legs were falling asleep, so I put her on our makeshift bed."

Combining all of their dirty clothes and backpacks from their journey, they had constructed one bed. The three slept on the floor, which allowed Marie to have the only cushioned area. That was when they slept. Gabriel wasn't sure, but he would have sworn the water was a stimulant, almost making sleep unnecessary. He knew he was averaging only two hours a day, but his body felt more alive than it ever had. He didn't mind not sleeping. His dreams were plagued by visions of his wife and son's violent demise, making the few hours he slumbered a hellish torment from which he would awake in a cold sweat.

With a youthful spring in her step Samantha hopped up onto one of the tables, and said, "Okay, test time." Gabriel and Othia both looked at her with a vacant expression that almost made her laugh. "You both have been studying for days. Let's see what you have. I promise not to fail you. After all, you both know the info a heck of a lot better than I do. Come on, Gabriel. You first."

Gabriel shrugged and looked to Othia, "We might as well get some practice in before the main event."

She nodded, and Samantha leaned back against a shelf resting atop the table, holding hundreds of books. She looked almost out of place. Young and attractive, she should have been out enjoying her youth, but so much had changed. Gabriel knew that a lot more people would soon be thrust into a violent war that many had no idea existed. Gabriel cleared his throat and said, "Okay, what would you like to know?"

"Well, let's start with something simple, something the new arrivals are going to ask. How about, why are we here?"

Gabriel grinned and took in an exaggerated deep breath, "Simple? Yeah, right! Okay, we have to go back to nearly the beginning. There is a story in the Bible that describes a tower being built, because mankind wanted to reach the heavens. Man had been cast out of the garden, and nearly wiped off the face of the Earth by the flood. From the information here, their motivation to get right with God again seemed to be their underlying drive. Their ambitions were manipulated and ill-inspired by those who wanted to see God's creation fail again. The first failure was rectified with the flood. You know Noah and the boat? Anyway, mankind flourished after the flood and with the aid of supposed otherworldly messengers, attempted to build a tower to reach Heaven. These divine beings turned out to be enemies of creation and not only led humanity astray but also nurtured sin among the masses. Those who saw a possible rapid punishment from the father were given false offers of protection from any wrath the Kingdom could bestow. The blasphemous nature of the tower and humanity's downward moral spiral drew the attention of the heavenly masses. Legions of angels, loyal to God, demolished the tower and killed all those involved. Since all of humanity had a part in erecting the tower, whether directly or indirectly every soul was held accountable. However most had been seduced by the fallen, and given false guidance and promises of protection.

When His wrath came in the form of His angels, those who had promised to stop such a reprisal faded from sight, leaving mankind to receive the entire wrath the legions of angels brought forth. The Father came down and saw what had happened. It was His decision to destroy the tower, but He had not ordered the eradication of His children. He didn't chastise the angels, for they were simply protecting His word, and so He decided that those who were not directly involved would forever be tasked and called His saints. All who were destroyed that day were brought back from the depths of Hell and scattered to the farthest reaches of the planet, their languages confused so Satan could not join humanity together to corrupt their number as a whole.

"Each of those chosen to be here has a bloodline link to those saints who were divinely singled out that day. With the passage of time, the bloodlines have stayed true but have become intermingled throughout all cultures. However, the signature on the soul has been bestowed at birth. Not every generation is called. In fact, the calling of the saints skips several generations, which has played a part in the unilateral ignorance of the bloodlines. This group of people is destined to battle the fallen, those angels who revolted against Heaven's will and were cast from the Kingdom. As I said, not every generation is called. It is only when the situation is dire and the legions of Heaven are in need of support.

"The saints can only be called thirteen times. Why only thirteen? Well, it is supposedly a power number—at least that is what the books say. Jesus had twelve always around Him, and if you count

Him, well, it's thirteen. The Jewish religion holds the number in high regard, too. There are many other inferences cited in these texts, but we are getting off course. This is the thirteenth time, the final call to stand ready to defend that which humanity holds most dear.

"Every society that has been called upon to gather the saints has foretold of the final time. The Toltec culture even gave the exact date when the final stage of the war would begin. I haven't found that yet, but I think Othia knows. Anyway, it's all in these books and parchments. Every culture, every epic civilization has documented its call and how their numbers were critical in thwarting the fallen. We are made in the image of the Father, the most prized of His creations, and we have been asked by the Son to protect what He has promised us. We have been called to keep Heaven safe so that entry into the Father's house, will be honored. That's what we are doing here and what lies ahead."

There was a pause, and Gabriel waited for a moment before he spoke again. "So, what do you think? Is it a good enough answer?"

Samantha's mouth was agape. She closed it and nodded, a blank stare etched onto her face. "I didn't know all that. I mean, I guess I did, but since I didn't hear it all at once—we need to think of a better way to tell people this. Do you think they'll believe us?"

Gabriel thought for a moment and then said, "I think they will. Something is driving them here. I don't think there won't be questions, but I think that if I tell them straight, they will know deep down that it's right and that they truly do have an important part to play. Come on. Ask another."

Samantha looked around the library for a moment and then smiled, "Sure, what's this place we're in?"

Othia smiled and said, "Ahh, an easy one. This is one of the strongholds that have supported the saints when the call has been sent. Seven altogether. There are several maps throughout the library, and each is exquisitely detailed. The strongholds may not all look like this, but each matches this location in size. The one we are in now was the third to be built.

"When the covenant was made with the saints, the angelic legions lent their support to ensure that the infrastructure would be sufficient to allow the small portion of humanity to cover the entire expanse of the world. Now that is not to say that we can influence what goes on around the globe—that is not our place—but we are strategically located throughout the planet so that if one stronghold is compromised, the others can still operate.

"The most well-known mention of these hidden locations is in the book of Revelation, where John writes to the seven churches. There are dozens of letters, books, and other documents in this library that show that John was actually writing to the commanders at each of the seven sites. Sometimes the best way to hide something is to put it right out in the open, and so he used the stronghold names. Each is equipped to provide food, water, and shelter, but nothing else. That is where the individual creativity of the given generation comes into play. Good enough?"

Samantha nodded. "Have you thought about the necessities yet? I mean, how are we going to get them?"

Gabriel shook his head, "I am letting that one play itself out. I am hoping that we sort of luck into something or that the solution comes to me when they arrive, but the bottom line is we aren't doing anything until after the first wave gets here."

Chapter 9

The Truth Will Set You Free—But to What End?

The potential of man should be understood and mastered. Favored above all in creation, our touch will set his world ablaze with the lust for power.
~ Gospel of the Babel 2:97

Location: Washington, U.S.A

Air travel was originally conceived to be luxurious and precise. The modern experience was anything but. With the invention of the layover, airline hubs and delays caused by an aging fleet, air travel was far more stressful than the epicurean experience it was intended to be. Handling stress was a perishable skill.

Standing by the baggage claim carousal Scott reaffirmed his mantra from his days in the military, to survive in the strangest and most life-threatening environments the world could offer, you needed to make stress a part of your life, never setting it aside. As he looked at the multitude of faces around him he knew he had unintentionally stepped back from the stresses of combat over the recent years.

Leaving the military machine had consequences. His senses were on overdrive attempting to identify, sort and prioritize everything they took in. He was not delusional; he knew he wasn't in a combat zone, yet every fiber of his being was on alert. His gut had never steered him wrong before; something was off.

He held Ann's hand after they retrieved their bags, weaving them through the crowd. She was placating him, hoping with each passing second he would come to his senses. Scott knew he couldn't make her understand, but he was going to keep her safe. Stepping out of the terminal he witnessed something that nearly made his heart stop. A man at the far side of the hotel bus waiting area made eye contact with him and then rapidly looked away. In his current state of panic, that alone would have been enough, however the man then put his hand to his mouth as though talking into a hidden microphone.

Scott wasn't an idiot; he could spot an inexperienced mistake. The fact that someone was watching them didn't bother him. Instead it solidified his mental state. He wasn't crazy after all and now he knew who the enemy was. Steering Ann into a cab and telling the driver to head toward Seattle, Scott was beginning to finalize his plan. They would hit the city, and rent a car there. Would it be enough to lose the tail? He would have to decide that later he supposed. Pulling away from the terminal he lost sight of the man in the business suit. That was unfortunate, but he could work with it. Each incident validated the horrific vision, increasing his conviction to keep his wife safe.

***

Commander Miller watched a collection of live streaming video feeds. Each of the twenty displays were the top of Red Horse's priority list. Orders had been specific and unyielding. Surveillance only, no overt action was authorized. Targets were to be identified by ground assets and then handed over to the aerial reconnaissance division for tracking.

On the surface the flagged travelers looked like a bizarre coincidence of multiple people wanting to vacation in Washington State. As data began to be compiled and cross referenced there was a definite pattern. Not in the demographic, race or sex of the travelers, but their behavior as well as their final destination. The first ten travelers flagged by the artificial intelligence algorithm monitor and placed under UAV surveillance had arrived at a remote location in the woods of the Olympic National Park. The AI was cross-referencing several data streams. It took into account everything from which kind of ticket and how it was purchased, to the location where it was bought, along with current behavior annotated by desk agents at check-in. As soon as the individual was flagged, TSA conducted an inventory of the traveler's belongings, and social media and phone records were scoured to see if the trip had been mentioned to anyone. Not one of the persons they were tracking had so much as called or sent e-mails to friends and family about their trip. From a strategic intelligence perspective this was an activation of countless sleeper cells within the Continental United States. Live overhead thermal video showed the number of people gathering together was far larger than just the names they had collected. Lines of cars of all makes and models lined the nearest road and it seemed more and more people were arriving by the hour.

Protocols would dictate a response. Tensions were high in the government, all of the agencies were jumping at shadows. A gathering of this size would draw the attention of the other agencies soon. He needed to compartmentalize this before the intelligence community reacted in counter intuitive ways. Using his secure phone he called the operations center responsible for data collection.

The call was answered immediately; a calm and professional voice greeted him. "Ops Center, this is Major Kline; how may I assist you Commander Miller?"

Clearing his throat Miller answered quickly, "Major, I am declaring a level 7 compartmentalization on Operation Shadow. All over flights are restricted to internal assets. National taskings are terminated; establish a red box cordon, I don't want over flights of any kind. Get me the new data feed sent to the executive suite. Only my team is involved now."

"Understood Sir, the new team comes on in twenty minutes, we'll have this locked down by then. Do you want the archived data transferred as well sir?"

"Yes, I'll expect the new feeds in fifteen minutes. Let me know if they are any issues."

With that he ended the call. The level 7 designation would give him time; it could only be overridden by this commander.

Fortunately for him, the Commander of Red Horse was overseeing operations in the Middle East for the week. Moving this to his team would keep it all under wraps. They knew where this strange collection of people was going; now they just needed to see what happened next.

He pulled an encrypted phone from this pocket and sent Cincaid a message. Her access through the Vault would allow her to monitor the situation to her satisfactory conclusion. They had a week to resolve the issue or it would require more direct intervention by personalities above his level of command. Typically the Assembled did not operate so openly. There were always instances where they applied more pressure to ensure their goals were accomplished, but never so direct.

This crisis somewhat contained, he shifted his focus to other sanctioned Red Horse Missions. In the world of espionage, appearances were everything. Hot button issues, and rash actions from Rogue States were a daily occurrence. Now he needed the Willis issue to be buried and forgotten by the masses. Only then could he leverage the situation to a desirable outcome.

Chapter 10
A Foretold Meeting

Contend, O Lord, with those who contend with me; fight against those who fight against me. Take up shield and buckler; arise and come to my aid. Brandish spear and javelin against those who pursue me.
~ Psalm 35:1-3

Location: *Ephesus*

Gabriel sprang upright; his sweat-soaked clothes clung to him as he woke from the deep recesses of a dream, allowing the images of his slumber to disappear. The blade on his back began to feel cold; an icy tingle that made his bones ache. The sword, a gift from his supposed allies in this war—was an ancient weapon that had protected the Garden of Eden for countless centuries, up until recently. He stood and removed the blade from its ancient scabbard. The weapon looked outwardly unchanged, but he felt a weight that had not been there before. There was a strange pull at the back of his mind, and he quickly sat back down with the priceless relic cradled in his lap. He looked over to make sure that Marie was still by his side and then closed his eyes.

He had been reading several passages from an ancient text compiled of the personal notes from previous commanders of the legion. The text was written entirely in angelic script so working through it was slow going. Its title translated to "The Legions Heart." This priceless work was invaluable to him, and one passage came flooding into his mind. He relaxed his body and began to breathe deeply, trying to slow his heart rate and focus on the blade in his lap. He sat tranquil for several moments, each breath measured and precise. The details in the book had been specific: how long to breathe in and how long to exhale. Everything had to be perfect for the link to be created.

"Very impressive, Gabriel. I was not sure you were open enough to explore a connection this early." The deep voice of Vicaro boomed in his head, and Gabriel's face grimaced.

"Tone down the volume, brother," he said. His head ached as though he was attending a heavy metal concert. There was a small chuckle in the depths of Gabriel's mind, and then Vicaro's quieted voice emerged back into the forefront of his consciousness. "It is time, Seraph. Your presence is required at the end of the east passageway. I have gathered the core of your flock. You must usher them into their new life." Gabriel sat for a moment. He was still trying to grasp the fact that he could communicate with Vicaro, not truly comprehending what was being said. "Gabriel, I need you to focus and move."

Gabriel remained seated for several breaths and then stood, his eyes still closed tightly. "Vicaro, where are you?" There was another roar of laughter, and Gabriel nearly fell to the floor from the staggering volume erupting in his mind.

"Gabriel, after all that we have been through, I never dreamt you didn't know the nature of our relationship. I am always with you, for my soul was fused to this weapon when I was chosen as the guardian. My life rests within the tempered blade, and I have either guarded Eden or aided the commanders of the Thirteenth for as long as I can remember."

Gabriel slowly stood and took in the new developments. He knew that the link between his angelic tutor had come from the ancient blade that he held, but he had never imagined the two were one and the same. "Deal with the reality of this new information later, Gabriel," Vicaro continued. "I have brought your warriors to you at the end of the east passageway. You need to usher them in."

"Vicaro, we still have two more days. They're not supposed to arrive yet." Another icy chill ran the course of Gabriel's body, and he began to move toward the east passageway. As his footsteps carried him across the center of the chamber, he felt the connection between himself and Vicaro slipping and then disappearing altogether.

Yeah, for another time, he thought. *Got it. This is getting out of hand—short-staffed, overworked, and now ahead of schedule. This was a nightmare in the making.* He left Othia, Samantha, and Marie sleeping. He was thankful that the others hadn't woken up to see him talking to the ancient weapon. Things were odd enough as they were. He didn't need them thinking he was going off the deep end.

It took him about ten minutes to reach the end of the east passageway, his ancient blade lighting the way with a blue flame that danced along its length. As his footsteps carried him into the small chamber at the end of the tunnel, he looked toward the rear wall and saw that there was no longer a ladder as in the antechamber, but rather a prodigious stone door. The frame was covered in angelic text, and the center of the door held his legion's emblem of the crescent moon. As he moved closer to the door, it slid silently open. Not a single sound was made as the large stone door swung cleanly into a tunnel behind it. Gabriel marveled at the sheer size of the colossal aperture and then walked through the doorway.

The passageway weaved back and forth through rock formations, but the path was unmistakable. He paused and sheathed his sword several feet outside the door when he overheard whispering voices. Gabriel stopped and listened. The acoustics in the passageway were terrible, and he couldn't truly hear what was being said. As quietly as he could, he crept around the corner and froze in his tracks. There, spread out before him, were at least two hundred people. The group was crowded in an outcropping of trees that rested just outside the opening to the passageway. He stood motionless for several moments, shocked at the sheer number of people sitting on the ground. There were families, and others who had come alone. Each person carried personal effects, but none appeared out of place. They all seemed to belong there in the dark woods, the only light coming from the full moon directly overhead. The faint glow added to the historic moment, and Gabriel swallowed hard before he walked out into the open.

As Gabriel stepped into the moonlight, all eyes turned toward him. There was a palpable calm in the air, and he looked at the assembled masses. "Hey, did anyone see where I parked?" he asked. The joke did little to placate the huddled people, and Gabriel nodded his head. "Yeah, I know...bad joke. Just trying to lighten things up. I don't know how all of you got here or what guided you to this spot, but I do know why you are here." His voice carried across the open area flawlessly, and he could almost detect a slight baritone hint coming to the forefront.

"My name is Gabriel, and we are all about to share in something truly remarkable. I am sure most of you are tired, hungry, and even a little frustrated. Come with me and let me try to make some sense of this mystery for you."

There was a slight hesitation, and a man stood up in the middle of the group. His unkempt appearance told Gabriel that he had been traveling for a while. "That's it?" he questioned. "You just want us to stand up and follow you? What are we doing here?" The man looked worn, nearly at his wits' end, his New Jersey accent thick and Gabriel saw the fear in the eyes of the woman sitting beside him. Her frantic looks left and right suggested that this topic had come up before.

"I can only imagine your frustration," Gabriel said, "and truthfully, I think you all would feel better and listen more intently if you had food and water. Maybe even a little rest. But I can understand your apprehension. It is not by accident that you all found your way here. You are the first of many to come to this spot, and while I was told to expect you and rehearsed a speech a thousand times, I can't say that any of those rehearsed remarks will even begin to stem the tide of questions you have. All I can say is you have come this far on blind faith. Take a few more steps and let me make you comfortable before I tell you where that faith has brought you."

The man stood defiantly still while others all around him began to move toward the entrance to the passageway. "Don't you all see what is going on? What are you? A bunch of lemmings? This doesn't make any sense. We all come out to the woods in the middle of the night, and this guy appears out of nowhere and tells us to follow him.

59

I'm sorry, but I have read my fair share of dime-store horror novels. And all the people get eaten in every single one I can remember. What is this? Some kind of Jim Jones Kool-Aid commercial?"

Gabriel laughed out loud and startled himself. This was all a little over the top—the moonlight, the hidden passageway, the fact that it probably looked as though he had stepped out of nowhere. He had to give this guy credit. It all did look a little too staged, and of course, his unkempt appearance did not help matters at all.

"You're right, to a degree. This is a little over the top, not what I had intended. Honestly, it just worked out this way. There are things that you don't understand, things that you couldn't understand, things that will keep me from telling you everything out here. But I promise you I will tell you everything inside. You have come this far. What have you got to lose? I think you all have me outnumbered, so you can't be nervous about me taking advantage of you. So here is the deal: if you want to come along or if this is where you feel your path ends, so be it. I will not force you to go any farther." The group was now beginning to press together, and Gabriel had to take a step back. He turned and walked into the darkness of the passageway, hoping that all of those huddled souls in the clearing would follow him into the safety of the stronghold. He could hear the man in the clearing still speaking and rationalizing the events that he had deemed important and vital to his assessment to the situation. Soon, his voice faded into the distance as Gabriel led the mass of people into the depths of the stronghold.

***

Scott sat silently, the oddity of the situation clamoring inside his mind. As he glanced around, he saw there were a few others who shared his skepticism. Ann captured his attention, gently caressing his leg. "It will get cold soon," she said. "I can feel it starting to set in now that everyone is gone. What are we going to do?"

Scott's initial reaction steered him back toward the rental car that had brought them to the middle of nowhere. Before his mind could solidify a course of action, a flash of his nightmare crept into his consciousness. He froze. An intense fear rooted him to the ground, and he feared his bowels would vacate. Ann's concerned expression pulled him from his horrifying reemergence into the hellish scene. Scott again felt the pull and grasped Ann's hand as he hurried after the mass of people. The sound of rustling in the vegetation told Scott the others who were undecided had come to the same conclusion that he had. Their commitment to the same course did little to quiet Scott's antagonistic feelings, but it did placate his concerns about his sanity.

Chapter 11

You Think Selling Your Soul to the Devil is Bad—Try Holding a Meeting with Him

Even though I walk through the valley of the shadow of death, I fear no evil for you are with me; your rod and staff, they comfort me.
~ Psalms 23:4

Location: The Schloss, Germany

The smell of musk hung in the air. Wavering torchlights sent shadows dancing off the smooth stonewalls of the subterranean chamber. Anger, distrust, frustration, and bloodlust coursed through the air like bolts of lightning. Covered in a lavish satin cloak, a lithe woman stepped out of the darkness, her thin body hidden in one of the multitude of alcoves that surrounded the massive chamber. Her eyes adjusted to the light and took in the subterranean room, a smile caressing her lips. The stiffness of her limbs and the subtle expression of bewilderment faded as the effects of a prolonged sleep left her body. She turned to look at the man and woman who now stood behind her, blocking the only exit to the vast circular opening in the earth.

The woman bowed deeply, her arms flaring from her sides, and then she said, "My Lord Uther, I am honored that you asked to hold a private meeting with me."

Uther didn't acknowledge her in the slightest, but the woman who stood next to him walked slowly forward. A black bodysuit covered her athletic frame. The tight-fitting suit held nothing for the imagination to ponder, there was only one woman with such confidence for such a bold seductive look. The woman in the cloak knew immediately that the figure in black was Cincaid. With piercing eyes Cincaid looked the woman up and down. The cloak that the other woman wore was open slightly, and the flashes of white skin told all who noticed that she was completely naked under the folds of the garment.

Cincaid's mind flashed to her private meeting with Uther hours earlier. The news of her recent failure did not go over well. Pain flared in her ribs where she had collided with the ground after Uther's strike, a blow that contained an unprecedented amount of force. The unbridled rage that danced behind his eyes still lingered in her mind. He was becoming more powerful with each passing day. She didn't even have a chance to tell him of the potential victory of the Devourer inside the temple. The acolytes were still working their incantations to try to establish a link. Time would allow the situation to develop.

Cincaid's mind shifted again, and her eyes took in the woman before her. Silently, the two women stood facing one another, "You know who I am?"

The slight caress of Cincaid's voice was smooth, it's harsh bite gone for the moment. The woman who stood in the black cloak nodded and said, "You are Uther's second, the bringer of death, the mistress of murder, and the protector of truth."

A smile crossed both women's lips, and Cincaid continued, "Say my name so that the demons who receive you in Hell will fear me before I arrive."

The woman in the black cloak tilted her head to the ceiling and cried as loud as her lungs would allow, "Cincaid!"

When her eyes settled back on the two figures, Cincaid was now kneeling before Uther. Her arms stretched upward, her palms facing the sky, cradling a bone-hilted knife. The black steel had been polished to such a shine that the flames of the torches could be seen wavering across the razor-sharp edge. Uther's gaze shifted from the blade to the woman before him, and he nodded solemnly before he said, "Your life is forfeit for the truth. The false promises of the Father will be cast down, and you will aid in that. Are you willing?"

The woman before him pulled at the cloak and let it fall to the floor. With sweat glistening off her nude body, she simply nodded and closed her eyes. Uther's hands tightened around the black knife, his fingers gripping the hilt tightly.

Cincaid stood slowly and positioned herself in front of the opening to the chamber, her eyes watching the practiced steps of Uther as he walked purposefully toward the willing sacrifice. The woman's eyes glazed over as Uther approached. She could hear soft murmurings coming from Uther but couldn't make them out. She knew that he had started the ceremony and that the room would soon be awash with his powerful voice. Uther raised the black blade into the air, catching the torchlight just right. Strange words shot from his mouth, filling the massive chamber with an animalistic quality.

Barks and howls leapt from his lips as his body stood rigid in front of the nude sacrifice. His hands quickly returned to his sides, and Cincaid could hear the powerful thrust as the blade entered the woman's stomach. The room became deathly silent as Uther pulled the blade up, slicing the woman open in one powerful pull. He turned and walked back to where Cincaid stood. The woman swayed back and forth, a distant look still etched on her blood spattered face, and then as though a light switch had been turned on, her face contorted into an anguish that Cincaid had rarely seen. A dying scream left her as her intestines fell to the floor. Her limp body soon followed. The sickening slosh echoed through the chamber. Uther walked calmly forward and dipped his finger in the pooling blood at the woman's feet. Slowly and deliberately, he drew two symbols into the dirt, allowing the blood to run its course and fill each of the symbols together.

Cincaid felt the undercurrent of energy as an invisible pulse of power shot to the ceiling and blood filled the rest of the symbol on the floor. Her eyes watered as she watched waves of smoke billow out of the ground, an omega with a nearly complete triangle in its center.

She knew the sign well; however, with each use of its power, she was still awed by the staggering strength that it held.

Tendrils of smoke lingered around the slumped head of the disemboweled body and then disappeared into the dead woman's nostrils. Cincaid watched as the blood in the symbol began to bubble and the temperature in the room began to rise slightly. The body on the ground shuddered violently and then lay still. The sound of cracking bones and snapping tendons rang out as the dead body shook again.

Cincaid felt Uther's strong grip on her shoulder, and she looked at him. A dark expression came over his features, and he held out the black blade. "Remain in the shadows. This will not be a pleasant meeting, and I do not wish to aggravate our guest any further by having too many people here. Remember where your loyalties lie, my dear." With that, he walked forward and stopped a few feet from the body, which shook with multiple spasms on the ground.

Cincaid did as she was told and grinned slyly to herself. She knew perfectly well where her loyalties lay. Uther was her everything, and nothing would ever do him harm, not while she still possessed the ability to do something about it. He was her savior. A life of privilege had kept the truth from her. She had been an empty shell before Uther had found her.

Deep within her soul she had felt a yearning, for what she didn't know. Her family's catering to each far-reaching desire exposed her to nearly everything humanity had to offer. Every endeavor to find her way, failing to satisfy more than the one before. When she met Uther that had all changed. His very presence filled her soul to nearly overflowing. At his command, she abandoned her family and life of privilege to pledge her unending loyalty to her new world, to the man she would now give her life to protect.

She moved into one of the alcoves and reached up to touch the center of the arch. Her fingers wiped away a lingering moss that had grown over a carved symbol. A slight tingle in her spine told her that the rune was free of the moss and that her presence would not be registered by the entity with whom her master was about to converse.

She backed into the small opening and felt the familiar pressure of the 9mm pistol she carried at the small of her back. Her mind raced with all the possible scenarios that could unfold, and she mused that all of them could be handled with the firearm or the bone-hilted knife. Then her eyes grew wide as the broken body began to stand.

Uther took an instinctive step back as the dead woman swayed perilously and tried to upright herself. Blood spattered on the ground as more fluids fell from the woman's dead flesh as it began to rise. A smile crossed Uther's lips as the woman's eyes shifted from the dull gray of the dead to a vibrant flame. The body shifted and shuddered again as it finally stood erect and looked around the room. Its dark and menacing eyes settled on Uther, and he bowed lavishly.

"I have news to share, and I didn't want to intrude on your personal activities," Uther said.

The animated corpse before him cackled. "The only news I wish from you is the whereabouts of our mutual enemy. You have accomplished what you promised, haven't you, favored son?" The woman's jaw didn't close, and a torrent of blood spilled from her mouth and covered her butchered front.

Uther took another small step back. "We have met with some unforeseen complications."

"Are not all complications unforeseen?" The tone of the dead woman was beginning to rise, and Cincaid felt a tingle in the pit of her stomach. Things were about to go very badly.

"You have come alone to bring me news of your failure? You have too much confidence in your abilities, mortal. My master may have once held you in high regard, but your failure has destroyed any chance of reward. I will see to your demise personally." The corpse uttered a strange sound, and it shook the chamber as though an earthquake had just struck. Cincaid watched as Uther's body went sailing through the air and smacked into the wall at the far side of the chamber. An insidious laugh filled the chamber, and the dead woman took a step toward Uther.

Cincaid watched as the intestines of the woman dragged between her reanimated legs, as she shuffled toward Uther. Razor-sharp bone began to protrude from the woman's fingers, and Cincaid tried to stir her master through sheer force of will. Nothing was happening, and with each passing heartbeat, the beast within the dead woman was getting closer. The possessed flesh-puppet froze for a moment as she felt Cincaid leave the shadows. "Not alone after all?"

Voices filled Cincaid's head as she crossed the threshold of the alcove, the protective symbol no longer disguising her as she departed. With a sudden heat-filled breeze, Cincaid's surroundings changed instantly. Concern faded away quickly as she saw herself standing at the front of millions screaming her name, their allegiance pledged to the insurmountable power given to her by the thing that possessed the body of the dead woman. Her mind was caressed with different possibilities of power, all of them so enticing that any normal person would have been enthralled, gladly condemning the entire planet for only a fraction of what she was being promised.

The sound of the dead woman shuffling again brought Cincaid out of her trance. She blinked and looked venomously at the demon, still moving closer to Uther. Cincaid's hands acted instantly, not wasting time with conversation. The pistol appeared in her hands, and she fired two shots at the dead woman's knees. Screams of frustration and rage filled the chamber as the bullets tore through the bone, making the limbs useless. Tissue and bone began to boil on the demonic form where the rounds had touched. Uther's body began to stir at the increased noise. The dead woman still tried to pull herself across the ground as Uther began to sit upright.

The fire in the dead woman's eyes flared brighter as she turned and looked at Cincaid, "I will take great pleasure in tearing the flesh from your bones. Your master will not be able to protect you forever!"

With the dignity of a wounded king, Uther pulled himself upright and then stood over the crawling dead woman. "You and I have an agreement. Never forget that. I see that your power is growing, but you will soon come to understand that our master favors me far more than you. It would behoove you to remember who brought you to this plane."

The body shifted again and pushed itself nearly upright so that the intense red eyes could stare at Uther. Bloodstained lips parted, and a dark look settled into the dead woman's face. "Do not presume to exert any authority over me, you parasite."

Uther bent down and grabbed the woman's chin and pulled her up to a more exaggerated angle, "I will call upon you when we have any new developments."

Uther released the dead woman's chin and simply opened his hand. Cincaid had been through enough rituals with Uther to know he wanted the black blade. Her hand gripped the knife tightly and then threw it expertly to Uther's waiting palm. The hilt of the blade landed perfectly in Uther's open hand, and in one fluid motion, he slammed the knife into the top of the dead woman's head.

A blinding flash of green light filled the chamber, fading almost instantly into a cascading mist. Uther walked over to Cincaid and pulled the pistol from her hand. His fingers worked nimbly, and he pulled one of the rounds out of the magazine. Strange writing covered the head of the bullet, and his eyes locked with hers.

"Where did you get this?" Cincaid was speechless for a moment, and she wavered a fraction of a second too long. Uther's hand was a blur, and before she could react, his palm slammed into the right side of her face. Cincaid crumpled onto the floor, the blow nearly causing her to black out. She looked up through blurred eyes at the towering form of Uther. "Your actions may have cost us years of planning. I need you to solve issues, not create them. I do not require protection. I am Uther, favored above mankind by the true master of creation. Never forget that, or you will find yourself a willing sacrifice for our next ritual."

Uther walked toward the door, hate still brimming all around him. Cincaid watched, and her eyes registered a shimmering heat rolling off his body, the way the sun's warmth rolls off a highway in the summer. Uther reached the opening of the chamber, and then he paused. Cincaid could see the waves of heat dissipating, and he turned to look at her. His eyes held power beyond her comprehension, and her body ached for his touch. "Find me something," he said. "Anything that will lead us wherever that illusive little shit is. I would suggest that you influence whomever you need to, so that thorn in my side surfaces and I can wipe him off the face of the Earth, or I will need to direct all my anger toward the person who failed me. Do I make myself clear?"

Cincaid nodded slowly and rose to her feet. She had seen Uther's rage before; this was a mild episode.

She understood her place in the hierarchy, and she knew that while Uther's temper was often the cause for most of the fatalities within the ranks of the Assembled, she was still in no danger. However, she was not willing to tempt her fate, and continued to remain submissive toward her raging master. Uther eyed her coldly and turned to walk away. An onlooker would have missed the subtle signal for Cincaid to join him; however, more than five years of loyal service had given them the ability to express themselves with simple gestures. She stood on wobbly legs and moved to join her master as he departed. She dragged her foot across the powerful symbol still smoldering with blood. She could feel the warmth of the charged bodily fluids seep into her shoes as she hurriedly joined her master in the dark confines of the passageway.

He stood silent for a moment and then looked at her, hate welling in his eyes. "Contact the acolytes and have them ensure the mark suffers. If the powers-that-be want to play rough, then by all means, we will make them victims of their own edicts."

Cincaid nodded, and together, she and he walked silently along the passageway, her mind swimming with the next task from her master. Time was against her. Uther wanted Gabriel's wife to suffer. The mark Cincaid had placed on the back of her neck acted as a conduit to funnel in the dark forces. The mark had gone silent almost fifty-eight hours ago. Cincaid would have to work quickly to bind Jennifer's soul for her master's dark purposes. Powers given from the false Father still could accomplish her dark plans. Time was against her. The ritual was complicated and costly, but his will would be done.

Chapter 12
Every Footstep We Take on Our Own is One Farther Away from the Father of Creation

In the last days, God says, I will pour out my Spirit on all people. Your sons and daughters will prophesy; your young men will see visions; your old men will dream dreams. Even on my servants, both men and women, I will pour out my Sprit in those days and they will prophesy. I will show wonders in the heavens above and signs on the earth below, blood and fire and billows of smoke.
~ Acts 2:17–20

Location: *Washington, U.S.A*

No one was witness to the blinding flash of light around a female physician in the sterile confines of the private intensive care unit. Mrs. Gionel's connection through the sacrificed member of the Assembled ended when Uther drove the dark blade into the host's skull. Residual pain radiated through her body as her consciousness fully returned. It had been an agonizing end to the ritual but worth it.

Surrounding her were the typical white walls of modern healthcare facilities. The false sense of security provided by the sterile appearance of the room went unnoticed by the inhabitants in their vegetative state. Mrs. Gionel's venomous eyes blinked and then took in their surroundings. Two still forms rested in a comatose state in pristine hospital beds. The invention of artificial life support had been intended as a temporary stopgap to keep patients alive long enough for doctors to repair damage in the body by means of surgery.

This marvel, however, had transformed into a way for loved ones to defeat death, or so they hoped.

Slender fingers danced on the rails of both beds. If the patients could have seen, they would have observed a seductive body swaying back and forth to an unheard musical melody. There was no sound in the room aside from the slow rhythmic rasps of the respiration pumps and the self-sufficient intravenous machines. Mrs. Gionel was beautiful to some and intoxicating to others but her beauty was simply a shell for an abomination that rested within.

The beast inside the slender form calmed itself. The failure of Uther, compounded by the pain inflicted by his pet bitch, coursed through her veins. A soft knock roused the woman from her trance, her silent footfalls carrying her to a solid wooden door, the only entrance to the windowless room. The door looked ancient, void of any seams, and somehow infused with a blackness that gave the visual impression that the tree had held this color during its life.

It opened without effort, and a young man stood in the doorway. "Mrs. Gionel, we have finished all the necessary paperwork, and these, along with five other patients, have been permanently moved to the floor." She nodded and stepped into the hallway. The floor seemed to be made of the same material as the doors, and the pair slowly walked down the hall.

Her aide, Walter, was one of the first to succumb to her dark gifts. She tolerated his over-attentiveness for only one reason: he had not yet failed her. The hallway they walked down was lined with fifteen rooms identical to the one that she had just departed. They were the final additions to the other thirty-four in the private wing. The hospital had an infinite amount of space for those who knew where to look. A covered stairwell in the basement led to an open area spanning the entire breadth of the hospital that rested above. Her unique influences had erected the secluded wings in short order, and her overly attentive lackey had worked diligently to populate it.

False death certificates, reports of unsuccessful surgeries, and the supposed accidental loss of documentation had served to relocate forty-nine coma patients from various locations to her private facility.

She found it utterly comical how trusting and uncaring humanity was. Families told of the passing of a loved one, and shown an official report, typically didn't want to see the body until the funeral. Those few who pressed the issue were crossed off the list and told the mistake had been with administration. Some of their numbers had come from homeless victims with no families to speak of, and so long as all the paperwork was filed correctly, no one cared.

The forty-nine patients were set into three groups, arranged in a half circle. The flooring and doors shared the black finish, while the walls within the hallways were covered in a marbled red paint. Mrs. Gionel found souls among the current staff that were inclined to her darker desires. Newcomers to the private basement section of the hospital felt dizzy for several days, until their minds adjusted to the maddening visual effect. Those who couldn't function due to the saturation of evil around them were never seen again. The dismissal and change-of-address paperwork was filed correctly to give the perfectly crafted illusion that all was well. There were forty-seven tending nurses and subordinate staff, Walter and Mrs. Gionel making up the last two, so that their numbers were identical to those who were resting in the beds.

The pair neared the end of the first group area, and her bold eyes turned to regard Walter before she said, "Have all my instructions been met?"

Walter nodded, his tone firm, "Every detail. We have even set aside the curriers as you described." Walter was a closet sadist, so her dominance actually excited him, and his mind was easy to manipulate with very minimal suggestion. However, Mrs. Gionel only valued his attention to detail. She had conquered and enslaved those with iron wills, but organization and a talent for perfection were not found in many, so those were the individuals on whom she focused.

Visually, nothing changed when they crossed into the next group of rooms, however, to Mrs. Gionel's senses, waves of intoxicating pain unabatedly flowed through the halls. This was what the majority of humanity was created for. They were not worth the gifts with which they had been showered. A dark smile crept across her face. Humanity would suffer. That was beyond question. But one man in all of humanity would suffer more than any other. His name was like a palatable pain as it formed on her lips. It came out in a harsh whisper as her mind's eye pondered the potential threat this man might become.

A solid thud slammed into the wall beside her. Something large inside the room had impacted the walls with tremendous force. "Show me the mature eaters," she commanded. Walter nodded curtly again and led Mrs. Gionel to the end of the current section of rooms. There, they stopped in front of a door similar to the one she had been in front of earlier. No markings adorned the smooth wood, yet she knew that Walter was unquestionably correct. The door swung outward, and as Mrs. Gionel looked inside, her lips parted in an evil grin. Her eyes glossed over with a thin, watery film. She blinked once, allowing the substance to be swept away. The room shifted as it came into focus.

The doorway remained the same, but the room inside had grown exceedingly large. Strange angles were evident in the new structure, because it reached high into an unseen ceiling. There were two hospital beds in the center of the massive room; however, the vegetative patients were no longer merely lying in a comatose state. Mrs. Gionel had altered her vision to see what was taking place in what some called, "the heavenly realms." Countless deformed creatures swarmed over the two patients secured to the beds. IV tubes and cables kept their bodies alive, acting as chains, holding them down as vile creatures tore great chunks of their soul free and devoured it. Sentry demons stood at evenly spaced intervals—more militant-looking creatures than the ravenous horde attacking the two victims. They were the feed controllers. They would pull the eaters back for only scant seconds to allow the soul to heal itself, and then the feeding would commence again. It was a vision of Hell on Earth— endless torment facilitated by the very advancements that were designed to usher in mankind's enlightenment.

Mrs. Gionel's eyes greedily consumed the chaos before her, her thoughts always envisioning the corrupt of humanity being devoured. The masses would yield to her influence soon enough. For she knew what was to come, and woe be to mankind, because the desolation coming over the horizon was horrific.

Chapter 13
Timely Assistance

With lasting faith and desire mankind will be elevated above us all.
~ Gospel of Babel 7:89

Location: *Ephesus*

Gabriel waded through the hushed mass of people as they crowded into the main chamber of the temple. He caught glimpses of their wide-eyed stares at the walls and ceiling and was struck by a strange feeling of impending doom. He tried to shake it off as he moved to the front of the crowd, but it lingered for too long and embedded into his mind. It tried to rise again, but he pushed the feeling back down as he turned and faced the people before him.

There was a small rise in the cavern floor, and it allowed him to stand a few feet above the masses so that they could all at least see him. "If I can get everyone's attention," he then said. "I know there are going to be a lot of questions from everyone. I will do my best to answer them all in turn, but first, let me try to answer some of them while everyone is here together. As I said before, my name is Gabriel, and like you, I have been brought here not by force, but not necessarily by my own free will, either." Gabriel's head swam. There was so much information he needed to pass on to them to help them understand, and though he had practiced this speech multiple times, he felt it slowly slipping from him.

"The place you stand in is a temple of sorts. A more appropriate word would be a stronghold. It has been used by our ancestors throughout human history as a staging point for waging war." There were muffled cries of alarm, and Gabriel could hear a rising tone of discontent in the crowd. "I have thought of how to say this for days, and to be honest, there isn't a good way to put it. But I swear I won't lie to you. Only the truth—you all deserve that much. Look around you. The walls, the ceiling—each depiction is of warriors battling unspeakable creations, things that should only be in the darkest places of our imagination; I want you to know that those things are real. The war is not amongst humanity but against the greatest enemy that our race has ever known."

"Oh, let me guess—the devil, right?" A small group off in the back began to laugh, and at least half of the group turned to look at the speaker set in their center. It was the man from the clearing again. "You want us to believe that you are building an army to battle the bogeyman. Ah shit, everyone, this is just some right-wing cult bullshit. Anyone ever hear of Waco or Jim Jones? This sounds awfully familiar." Cries of agreement erupted from the crowd, and Gabriel held up his hands for quiet.

"I know it sounds off-base," Gabriel said. "Really, I do. I didn't believe it myself, but I swear it's true. There are things that you will see, things that no one should ever have to see, but that each of you have been chosen to witness."

"Chosen by whom? You? What did you do? Pull our names out of a phone book?" The questions were beginning to affect the mood of the crowd, and Gabriel was rapidly losing what little trust they had given him.

All the questions were right. It did sound crazy, and no rational person would believe this without proof. A deafening crack echoed in the massive chamber, and everyone involuntarily crouched toward the ground—everyone except Gabriel. Gabriel looked to his left and saw the familiar signs of the lifestream begin to appear, and he looked back toward the mass of people.

"You want a sign to see that I am not some religious nut?" Gabriel asked. "I don't blame you. I would want one as well. Look over there, and your request will be answered in a second. Cover your ears. This may unnerve some of you." The vocal blast akin to thousands of children crying out echoed in the chamber, and Gabriel watched as a massive angelic form exited from a blackness that appeared from nowhere, and stood before the altar in the center of the chamber. The ways in which the angelic warriors traversed God's creation were completely foreign to him. His recent journey had exposed him to many things that he still didn't have real answers for.

The *lifestreams*, as they were called, allowed persons to move from one location to another almost instantaneously regardless of the distance between the two points. Samantha had stated that such a phenomenon was called a *wormhole* in the academic arena. But that wasn't what Gabriel set his eyes on now. There before the mass of people stood the proof that he needed to show the new arrivals. White wings spread in a display of pure majesty. The huddled masses instinctively knew the heavenly being was a warrior. Its body was twice as large as any man's and was encased in an exquisite suit of armor. Strange writing swirled around the suit, which made it appear to be alive, as the people looked at the creature in silence. The light from the chamber glistened off his polished gray armor, and the warrior looked around. When his eyes reached Gabriel, the warrior fell to one knee. "My apologies, Seraph," he said. "I did not know you would be addressing your warriors. I have come unannounced, and for that, I have no excuse."

Gabriel jumped down from the small rise and quickly walked over to the warrior, "Your timing couldn't have been more perfect if we had planned it."

The warrior looked quizzically at Gabriel for a moment, and then he stood, his eyes scanning the group before him. The angelic warrior's hard gaze lingered on the new arrivals and he simply gave them a curt nod and turned to face Gabriel again. "My name is Percious, Seraph. Semyaza has sent me to assist you in training your legion. He felt it wasn't advantageous for you to take on the challenge alone."

Gabriel frowned slightly at the presumed insult and then let his pride fade away. Semyaza was correct, and that much at least he would give him. "Smart man. I won't say I can't use the help. I don't think

I would have done them justice in close combat anyway. I don't think I got a strong training regimen, more of a learn-as-you-go refresher."

Percious's eyes grew narrow, and then he asked, "Your lessons were from Vicaro, correct?"

Gabriel nodded and then he smiled. "I think I got the rushed course. Events were transpiring faster than we could—"

The exchange looked like a blur to the huddled masses watching, but to Gabriel's newly gifted eyes, he registered all the events easily. His body stood still as Percious pulled a large halberd from his back and swung the weapon up to try to cleave Gabriel in half from the bottom up. The move was awkward, but the speed at which it was accomplished gave it a fluidity that impressed Gabriel. His reflexes took over, and his body contorted sideways to narrowly miss the rising blade. The sword on his back leapt into his hand, and as Percious recovered to make another swing, he paused and stood stone still. Gabriel held the tip of his sword centimeters from Percious's exposed neck. The angelic warrior raised an eyebrow and said, "Your training was better than even I expected, and your reflexes are honed so sharply that you truly don't know the power you possess. I will help you with that, Seraph."

Gabriel saw the group to his right in peripheral vision. The interaction had taken only an instant, and if anyone had blinked, they would have missed it, but he knew that none of them had. Whether Percious knew it or not, he may have saved the legion before it had even had a chance to exist. The murmurs had stopped, and all looked at Gabriel as he clasped hands with the mighty warrior that seemed to have appeared out of nowhere. Gabriel walked back to the rise and looked out on the sea of people before him. No one spoke, each of them waiting for his words as though their very souls depended on it—and in truth, he supposed they did.

The rest of the meeting went rather smoothly. Samantha, Othia, and Marie joined Gabriel after the lifestream sealed, and they knew Gabriel had things well in hand. Othia had insisted they stay hidden to let Gabriel set the tone for the first meeting. Marie even remained calm, her eyes never leaving her father as he talked to the large group. Gabriel walked them through the basics without interruption and showed them the map on the altar, which could guide them throughout the stronghold. He didn't mention the dark room and thought to keep that quiet—for now at least.

The newcomers were separated into three groups and then shown where the sleeping area was. Gabriel, Othia, and Samantha took turns walking groups of people down to the well so that everyone could get something to eat and drink. After the first few trips, they all became self-sufficient. Those who had already been shown the path started walking other new arrivals down. Gabriel found himself cornered most of the night, answering questions. Samantha and Othia would help him with Marie after she had fallen asleep in his arms. Her youthful thoughts had been genuinely disinterested in the conversation, but she was not willing to leave her father's side. All of the newcomers seemed so energized, the wonders contained within the stronghold captivating their attention; however their excitement soon turned to fatigue, and many moved to stake out an area in the vast sleeping chamber.

Gabriel pulled away from the clamor of questions and wide-eyed stares to talk with Percious. The angelic warrior was seeing to his weapons and armor near the dark room and seemed unaware of the attention directed at him. They conversed briefly, and though Gabriel knew that the warrior wanted to keep talking, he excused himself as a large group began to gather behind them, waiting for his attention. Gabriel watched out of the corner of his eye as Percious moved to a more secluded corner of the main chamber and began to readdress his armor as well as his weapons and relax slightly.

The questions lasted until morning. Gabriel was astonished at how few repeat questions there were. He had heard discussions in the sleeping area when he walked past small groups in his rare pockets of free time. People were passing along their questions and his answers, spreading the information like a wildfire. Most of the statements were correct. Very few embellished anything, and he only caught a few minor inconsistencies.

He saw Samantha heading toward the library, and he walked slowly behind her. She paused for a moment and then turned, gently smiling at him. "You're awfully spry for answering thousands of questions. I think my mind is about to explode, and I only know a little. I don't even want to imagine what your head must feel like right now."

Gabriel smiled. It was true. His head was pounding, but he knew it would go away in a few hours. The day hadn't fallen apart, and now with at least some people here on his side, the subsequent days would be somewhat easier—at least that was what he told himself. "Yeah, I got a headache. What I wouldn't give for a bottle of aspirin. I am going to sit with each group and talk about all the different dangers we are going to face tomorrow. I want you there so we can all talk about families, friends and supplies. I don't want only one view. You have been down here just as long as I have, so you have equal say for ideas on stuff we need to address."

Samantha nodded, a clear sense of purpose settling onto her face as though her involvement was critical to a successful meeting, which was what Gabriel had intended. They were all in this together, and everyone needed to feel included.

Samantha looked playful again and said, "Looks like you have another meeting."

Gabriel held his posture. His shoulders wanted to slump, but he knew it would send the wrong message. He turned and walked toward the small group of twelve. He had been talking with that group a lot, Samantha had noticed, and made a mental note to ask him about that whenever time allowed him to take a break.

Chapter 14
Whatever Action I Take, let it be for the Greater Glory of God!

The armies of the fallen will be bountiful, their atrocities unspeakable and their lord will praise them for it.
~ Gospel of the Babel 4:32

Location: Ephesus

Stephen James's eyes flew open, his heart beating so loudly and strong that his body felt as though it were swelling. Images swam through his head, blurred memories of pain and suffering. The smell of rotting flesh and human waste clung to his nostrils, unwilling to join the mental pictures as they faded into his subconscious. Sweat drenched his body, and his mind gripped firmly to one image that would not leave his mind's eye—the image of a young woman sitting in a dilapidated building, surrounded by childlike demons.

His head ached, and he tried to sit up. His hands being secured to a table leg hindered the process, and he simply laid back down. How much time had passed, and where was he? It looked like some sort of ancient library. He caught sight of a brief flash of movement to his left, and he tried to speak; however, all he got for his efforts was a croaked whisper: "Water." It was enough, and he saw the face of the man he knew as Gabriel appear over him.

"Awake, huh? Well, let's sit you up. I bet you're as stiff as a board."

He was right, of course. Even with the help, James's muscles ached as Gabriel helped him into a sitting position. Gabriel produced a small cup of water and slowly held it to James's mouth. The refreshing liquid seemed to supercharge his innards, and James felt his headache fade into nothingness.

"What's going on?" James asked.

Gabriel looked at him for a moment and then frowned, "What's the last thing you remember?" Gabriel watched as James searched through his mind for the answer and then sighed.

"A woman changing into that awful thing and then falling to the floor."

"Well then, you haven't missed much. You were waving your gun at all of us, so we shot you with a crossbow. The bolt hit you in the leg, and you have been knocked out ever since. You know, that whole fight-or-flight stuff."

James nodded in agreement. Everything was happening too fast. Questions flooded his mind, and he fought to regain some kind of control. "Are these necessary?" James asked, and pulled at the restraints.

Gabriel shook his head. "I think you are pretty sound right now, but sorry, I am going to have to keep the gun for a bit. I'm sure you understand."

In truth, James didn't understand, but there was little use in arguing the subject. He needed to get mobile and start gathering some information. Things were downright crazy right now, and if he was going to help himself, he needed to see what was going on. Gabriel pulled him to his feet and ducked under James's arm to help him walk. James let out a few pained hisses as they walked toward the door but continued on, determined to see where he was and make an assessment of his situation.

"My partner? Matthew?"

Gabriel heard the distress in the man's voice. "He didn't make it. He was too far gone." Gabriel held a tone of reverence. Their entry into the stronghold had been a convergence for each of their journeys. Both James and his partner found themselves in the middle of a demonic attack. Matthew had tried to rescue Gabriel's son before the creature his wife had turned into gutted the small child. The horrific bloodied affair marked the true activation of the Thirteenth Legion but it had cost all of them dearly.

James continued to rely on Gabriel for balance as the two made their way into the main chamber. The sight of the vast expanse and all the murals on the walls sucked the breath right out of his lungs.

"Yeah, it seems to have that effect on everyone." Gabriel tried to keep things lighthearted, but he could see the strain in James's face and thought better of further jokes. "Look, a lot has happened since our altercation outside. We both lost loved ones and people important to us, and we need to move past that. This is going to sound strange, but you are supposed to be here, James. There's a lot to digest, and I will answer everything I can. But you need to take things slow."

James looked at Gabriel and saw the sincerity in his eyes and nodded. "Okay, let's say for the moment I believe you—mind you, that is a big if—what's this place?"

"It has a lot of names, but the easiest way to describe it would be to call it a stronghold."

James hadn't even completely digested the information before he asked, "From what?"

Gabriel paused and thought for a moment and decided there was no nice way to say what was on his mind, "From things like what killed my son and your partner."

The two stood quietly for a moment, allowing the information to sink in, and then James urged them forward, "Why here? Why now?"

"That is a little more complicated. We are not the first to come here. In fact, we're said to be the last. Each of us carries a unique lineage to a set of ancestors who were chosen by Christ Himself to do miraculous things."

James scoffed, but Gabriel ignored it and continued, "Twelve times in the past, our ancestors have been called upon to fight with the armies of Heaven. It seems that the devil is obsessed with taking over the place, and when push comes to shove, there just isn't enough manpower to keep all his hordes from toppling the Gates of Heaven. There are frankly too many of them and not enough good guys, which is why we are here now. Short of going into every detail, we have been chosen to form an army, to wage war against the damned and protect the Gates of Heaven from being overrun."

James's mind rejected the idea outright as his eyes glanced around the chamber. He stared in astonishment. There were people down here. Not the small group he had surprised outside but hundreds, he guessed. James was about to speak, but Gabriel held up his free hand and said, "I know it is a lot to believe, but there is someone who I want you to meet that I think will help in that department." The pair shuffled through half of the cavern, and with each step, James got stronger.

Gabriel steered them to the far side of the main chamber, where a lone figure was kneeling in some form of meditation. Gabriel stopped their progress for a moment and then faced James before asking, "I've got a question for you. When you look at me, what do you see?"

James seemed perplexed for a moment and then shifted his eyes to the ground. "I don't know what you mean. Am I supposed to see something?"

Gabriel stood and waited for James to look up, and just as he had suspected, James squinted when their eyes met, as though he was looking at a bright light. "Samantha was right," Gabriel said. "You can learn a lot from her. After our little visit here, there are a few things you should read."

James didn't respond for a moment and then regained his composure. "A light. You're surrounded by light. What is it?"

"I don't know, but you have it around you too. Everyone here does."

"No, yours is brighter. It's blinding."

"That's because he's part of the seraphim." Both Gabriel and James jumped as the deep voice of Percious surrounded them.

Gabriel had to steady James to keep him from falling over when he craned his neck to try and take in the enormous figure before them. James struggled to try and mentally comprehend what was happening all around him. "A new arrival, Seraph?" Percious asked.

"Not exactly. You might say he's awakened. Percious, this is James. He's a seer without a mark."

Percious's eyes darkened, "Interesting. I have heard of those traits residing in humans but have never met one who possessed such a power. Tell me, James. What is it that you see?"

James looked at the ground and then began to fidget. Gabriel held his hand up to Percious when he noticed the warrior getting impatient. "Give him a minute. He really did just wake up."

James cleared his throat and then said, "Light. I see light."

Percious frowned and said, "Your gift is undisciplined, but I will help you, James. Soon, you will see what many among your kind wish they could keep concealed. You will see the true essence of mankind's soul."

James' balance wavered for a moment, and then Gabriel nodded his head. "I think that is enough for one day there, big fella. Let's get you back to the library for some quiet time." James didn't protest as he stood. His world was spinning, and if it weren't for the steadying shoulder of Gabriel, James didn't doubt he would be sprawled out on his back, letting the world spin around him. Percious and Gabriel exchanged nods of respect, and then they all went their separate ways.

Chapter 15
By My Own Hand

They must no longer offer any of their sacrifices to the goat idols to whom they prostitute themselves.
~ Leviticus 17:7

Location: The Schloss, Germany

The taste of blood soured her stomach. Cincaid sat motionless, her mind reaching out into the abyss. Her meditation was entwined with a black magic ritual. Stories from the past concerning events like the inquisition efforts to purge corruption from the masses were partial truths. Incidents such as the trials at Salem were a diversion. The purge was a carefully concealed war for secrets.

Throughout human history one truth remained a constant. Those in power would fight to preserve it. This has ensured the wealth of the world rested disproportionally with the top one percent of the population. Yet even among this elect group there was another power struggle. For the old axiom "money isn't everything" was very true. It had taken time, but for the last 300 years the Assembled were at the Apex of humanities power hierarchy. That placement was never challenged, all due to the secrets it possessed.

We are all a product of the teaching we receive. While Cincaid employed state of the art technologies to ensure her lord's wishes were fulfilled, her dark ritual performances were shaped and molded by her teacher, Uther. The complex ritual she was engaged in had been perfected during the dark ages and had been the conquest of the Church for decades. The Assembled kept it safe to ensure Rome never attempted to regain its lost influence upon the world.

As with all dealings with the fallen, and their underlings there was a fee with any interaction. There was never an accruing of collateral, each interaction stood upon its own. Here upon the dirt floor with her master forty-feet above her safely inside his private chambers she sat surrounded by a pentagram. Each of its points accented with the severed head of a newborn lamb. The delicate balance between subtle and blatant blasphemous behaviors was in constant flux; each dark being demanding to be catered to in different ways.

Her mastery of the dark arts was nowhere near Uther's; that is not to say she was without talents. Amongst the multitudes of the Assembled members she was second to Uther in skill. Even with such a large gap between their proficiencies she was granted complete access to the archives, which the secretive group had collected since its inception.

Through these closely guarded works she had learned of the Devourer. This dark entity scavenged upon the planes of the damned. A horde demon, it divided its consciousness among many physical forms. Each was an amalgamation of several predatory animals, yet its patchwork assembly was extremely sickening to behold. While not as powerful as many of the fallen, the Devourer's ability to multi-task with a high degree of success was its most desirable attribute. As with others of its kind it was the head of its pack, and could manifest a small army of demonic abominations if needed. A time worn communication between two power players from the age of the inquisition held an annotation explaining how a demonic entity named the Devourer had eyes everywhere. It was that single passage which prompted her months of study and ultimate summoning of the dark beast.

That ever-present gaze is what she needed now. CS's report had been a bitter pill to swallow. Now she needed any information she could get about where Gabriel had crawled to. Since the formation of their group, the Assembled had searched for the location of the gifts to humanity. A mythological stockpile of untold treasures. Now with modern technology they possessed a solid chance, yet as was the case with all ventures…time was against her. A reoccurring point she found during her study of the site called Ephesus was that the entrance to the treasure was only accessible for a short period of time. In the past that nuance had acted as a deterrent for further study. Now with the thermal imagery, ground penetrating radar, modern construction equipment, and dark magic, they had a true shot.

She calmed her mind and focused on cutting through the abyss to find the wounded Devourer. Her body was slick with perspiration as her face scrunched with effort. Projecting a mental summons into the abyss she received a faint echo of a reply. As she listened, Cincaid realized it wasn't an echo, but rather multiple child-like voices talking over one another. Their replies to her summons was erratic almost in a panic. Ask, ask, ask, you desire, our cost is specific.

Cincaid smiled, that was good, the demonic entity wanted something. That would make the exchange easier. She pictured Gabriel in her mind and projected her question. Where is he?

A shrill laughter erupted from the demon. Ephesus, Ephesus, Ephesus. One got through but was slain. The Seraph is in the temple.

There was silence as Cincaid pondered the information. Before she could articulate another question the Devourer spoke. We want the woman. Give us the woman. Give us the mother. GIVE US OUR MOTHER!

The exchange was becoming clear to Cincaid. Apparently, the Acolytes possession tag had activated when Jennifer entered the hidden temple. If Cincaid understood what the demon was saying, the incident had resulted in her death. Cincaid nodded, this could benefit everyone. Pushing her mind back into the abyss.

Very well, you wish to have the woman, we will bind her, how long until she ascends?

The voices came back instantly, one moon rise and then her soul departs this plane.

Cincaid accepted the terms, if the beast wanted a new plaything that was fine. She had the corroboration she needed. Now the question remained, what was she going to do about it.

Chapter 16

Motives Unclear

An oracle is within my heart concerning the sinfulness of the wicked. There is no fear of God before his eyes.
~ Psalm 36:1

Location: Port Angeles, Washington USA

Vermin such as the—Rattus rattus— or common black rat, were created to beat the odds. At a primal level they were always moving, always gnawing, constantly exploring the world around them. For a demonic envoy like Mrs. Gionel, such a creature had many uses. The rodent's single-minded focus allowed her easy manipulation and dominance. They were her eyes and ears within her growing domain. Collecting the information they gathered was problematic.

Two colonies lurked in the substructure of the hospital. The larger of the two groups always had a small cluster of their number around her. The bond between master and familiar needed to be fostered. She ensured that she always had a large collection of the rodents around her to ensure the link took hold within the colony.

As she waited for this bond to mature she used the smaller swarm's rodents individually to collect information. One of the small colonies four-footed spies lingered by her feet. Scooping up the furry rat she bit into its neck. It died silently; the normal primal will of the rodent was noticeably absent from this controlled vermin. There was an instant barrage of images and sounds that hit her senses. She would have to sort through them to make sense of the jumbled sensory inputs from the rodents blood. Until the bond with the larger colony was solidified she would have to do things manually. It wasn't pretty, but it worked well enough.

The fragility of the human body astounded her. Her true form was powerful, eternal and dangerous. It would take time for her mortal shell to be capable of containing even the slightest fraction of abilities she employed upon the planes of Hell. The conduit aided in the strengthening of her mortal frame. It was a beneficial side effect to being so close to the thin veils between realities. Her mission would be aided by a simplistic plan which required her to be within the depths of the hospital. Here in the shadows she could maintain a tight grip upon her legion, ensuring she could usher them across an artificial rift when the time was right. Such an ambitious goal was hinged on one pivotal key factor—control.

Her reign upon the planes of Hell was an unending existence of war. Her rule was not governed by ideologies, or grand promises to the masses, but by an iron fist clinching a gore slick sword. The conduit would allow her to still actively monitor her legion and her second in command. Treachery was lethal among the fallen angels and demonic spawn. Exerting her will over the fifth legion would be difficult in this form. Her consciousness divided, she existed upon humanities realm to accomplish a nearly impossible goal while her tangible shell still sat immobile atop her throne of suffering. Guarded by the elite of her legion she looked to be in a deep meditative state, but while she portrayed a visage of impregnability, she was vulnerable.

As she strengthened the bond between realities she could move artifacts. Ushering over items, which would allow her to accomplish her task. In her diminished state this simple act would force her to employ age-old rituals to enable her to create the bridge to Hell. While Uther and his pet were a triviality to her, the summing rite, which had brought her into humanities realm, constricted her powers. Akin to a heavy chain, the incantation limited her movement, not only physically but in the ethereal realm as well.

Now she would have to summon the only being within her legion she trusted. Loyalty, was fatal in certain circumstances, and she was creating a level of uncertainty by allowing Balbizar to be the proxy ruler in her absence. It was a calculated risk. There was little she could have done to avoid the summons. Only the Morningstar could have given Uther the incantation to bring her into their service. The strategy had been discussed following the damned's last unsuccessful attack upon the gates of the kingdom.

The alignment of celestial events had to be perfect for any member of the fallen to return to humanities realm. When her feet had last graced the mortal plane the tower had been destroyed. Mankind's ambition to reach the heavens was crushed in a decisive strike by the council of angels.

Her hands moved precisely, each bend of a finger, and twist of her hands was integral to the ritual. The manipulation of creation was an impossibly complex affair, designed to prevent any accidental or unintended consequences from affecting its delicate balance. Her body perspired and ached from the effort. As she added the complex vocalization of the ritual the air around her reeked of death and decay as the barrier thinned.

A deep guttural growl echoed around the room as a bestial head materialized within a plume of smoke. The thick cloud manifested in the center of what the hospital staff had once regarded as the storage area. Mrs. Gionel cleared her thoughts, allowing the spectral image to sharpen. A snarl greeted the demonic envoy as Balbizar locked eyes with the mortal shell before it. Wet, sloppy speech shook the room as torrents of drool vanished as it shot from the smoky visage. "My liege, I have missed your ferocity against your subjects. Yet the hordes are unaware of your departure and the accords with the ninth and eleventh legions are still resulting in only internal skirmishes against our forces transpiring upon your lands. How may I serve?"

The connection was at the limits of her abilities at the moments. She paced as her eyes looked on her second in command. "The limitations of these sacks of meat is wretched. I have need of my quills. The Morningstar will wish to hear of our progress soon."

Balbizar turned his head as though looking for the items she requested. The bestial head locked eyes with her again as he spoke. "I have them, do you wish me to place them into the abyss for you to recover or do you have a different plan for bringing them to you?"

Tangible objects were as difficult to pull between realms as living beings. Balbizar's suggestion was a way to circumvent the barriers, but her quills could be lost if she couldn't collect them without incident. Traversing the abyss was never incident free. She shook her head, "No we will have to use a more permanent means to transport. I have erected curriers, their bodies tethered to both realities. Place them within the chest cavity of the elderly man and I will recover them. The act will kill the weak vessel, but I can make more. You will find him where the conduit bridges through, erect a reflection to ensure the barrier remains thin."

The demonic warrior nodded in understanding and remained silent for any further instructions. When none were forthcoming the smoke separated and disappeared. Her orders given, Mrs. Gionel exited the storage room. A line of rats waited for her in the hallway, their minds filled with information she desired. Distracted she made her way to the intensive care area to await her quills. The rat she held in her hands remaining unnaturally still as she tore into its throat and devoured the secrets it had gathered.

Chapter 17
Each Path Given to Us from the Creator is Unique

The gifts, which our Lord has bestowed upon man, will be a mystery to us. His unconditional love and desire to love his chosen children will confuse us till the end of time.
~ Gospel of Babel 17:64

Location: Ephesus

The dream would waver maddeningly—colors, shapes, angles holding for a fraction of a second and then swirling away again. James fought for control. This had happened every night since he had awakened in this underground place. Life had taken on a new perspective after he found himself in the middle of a war. At first he had written the dreams off as a by-product of his mind struggling to rationalize his current situation. His soul was in constant battle with his analytical thoughts. This was his proper place—he knew it. However, a simplistic feeling wasn't enough to quench the mounting cries from his mind to leave this insanity and embed himself back into society. The dreams seemed to be the perfect argument, and an unrelenting one at that.

As he felt on the verge of totally losing perspective, his vision snapped into place. The effect was almost as disconcerting as the rapidly changing world before him. A red haze filled his eyes, and the landscape before him came into focus.

Bloodstained earth surrounded him. The darkening red sky held his attention for a moment as black clouds sent lightning streaming toward the cracked ground. What he assumed was a dried-out riverbed lay directly in front of him. He watched as he was propelled forward, simply hovering just above the ground.

He shuddered mentally as a woman whom he had seen for over a week within what he assumed was a tattered orphanage, stood chained to the bottom of the dry riverbed. She was thin and frail with a look of terror, pain, and exhaustive suffering etched onto her face. Her body was bare, her flesh covered in sores and crisscrossing scars. It gave the illusion that her body had been put back together so many times it didn't fit right anymore. James struggled with his own mental images of what the woman now looked like, then realized he didn't know if this was real or just imaginary.

A deafening boom shook the ground and drew his attention off to his right. The woman in the streambed was screaming now—the panicked, stricken shrieks of someone who knew what torment was about to befall her. James felt his head turn back toward the screaming woman. His mind tried to focus on something else. His eyes locked on hers as they always did. She looked right through him, but he understood somehow that the woman knew he was there. A sound like a rushing train hit his ears. Deep in the depths of his being, he knew his dreams would now be forever populated by the woman's new fate, and it would always be the same.

A bloody tidal wave slammed into the woman a moment later. The chains holding her securely in place didn't stop the current from tossing her around like a rag doll. The woman regained her footing as the water rose to her thighs. He instinctively knew it would keep rising. Eventually, the blood would drown her.

The viscous fluid began to boil around the woman, and her screams filled his ears again. Bright red tears began to appear on her white skin. The image before him shifted slightly again, and he could see what was causing her agony. Strange creatures the size of large dogs crawled over her, tearing and consuming her flesh bit by bit. The blood river began to rise again, and her cries were muted for a moment. The creatures disappeared into the raging torrent of blood. James could see torn muscles and exposed bone in multiple places on the woman's frail shell of a body.

He struggled against whatever force held him there. He needed to help the woman somehow. Another set of screams came from her, and James saw a strange insect swarm within the blood gathered around the woman, as the current swept her down the river. Their clawed appendages lashing out at her, tearing at eyes and taking more flesh from her tortured frame. James endured the sight of the woman's demise only a few moments longer. The current of blood soon swallowed her destroyed body, her empty eye sockets still pleading for help as the river of blood swallowed them.

James awoke violently; sweat covering his body, a terror-filled cry leaving his lips. Shaken to his core, he felt his hands tremble. He had seen his fair share of suffering as a police officer. Over twenty years of service had exposed him to countless acts of cruelty and accidents with horrific results. Yet none could compare to the terror of the dream.

He had fallen asleep in the library again. Othia was beside him in an instant. Her eyes asked all the questions. James nodded and said, "Yeah, bad dream, a real whopper." James saw Othia about to ask more questions, but he shrugged his shoulders and continued, "I know I've had a lot. Guess it is just my mind coping with everything." He sighed, Othia's expression was one of compassion.

James didn't know what the dreams were about, but they scared the crap out of him. He wasn't going to explore them any more than he had to—a kind of ignore it and hope it goes away approach. It hadn't worked in the past with emotional stress. Twenty-two years on the job would do that to you, but there was a first time for everything. At least that was what he told himself.

James refocused on the stacks of books around him, and a nearly defeated look crossed his face. How had he come to this?

Everything was such a blur. The severity of the situation he was in now struck him like a Mack truck with each new development. Flashes of news reports and morning briefs back at the police station filled his mind. They had all been shown pictures of Gabriel and told of all the heinous things he had done. Many were stomach-turning. He knew now that they had all been a lie, but seeing what the man was tasked with created more uncertainty and muddied the waters of his mind even further.

James knew he was not the smartest man on the planet, but like most, he had his days. He excelled in things because he worked tirelessly and never quit. His word meant more to him than anything, and he had given it to Gabriel, the terrorist, the last hope for humanity, the husband of the woman James had killed. He found himself in the one place he hated, the unknown. He wasn't kept in the dark. He met with Gabriel nearly two or three times a day. The enormity of the situation rested heavily on all of them. Angles, temples, demons, and now the whole raising-the-army thing were nearly too far over the top. Yet deep in the dark recesses of James' soul, he knew this was right. He needed to be here. This was something grand, and he had been tasked to see it through. No one needed to convince him of it. James simply needed to trust his gut, and that was going to take time.

Othia glanced at the rows of books James was combing through. "This is a very broad spectrum of information," she said. "Are you looking for anything specific?"

James looked down at the books and sighed. "To tell you the truth, I don't know really how to look for anything. Heck, I thought all these were part of the same subject matter—"

The sheepish grin made Othia smile broadly. "Nope, sorry, they are not even close. Why don't you let me help you? What are you looking for?"

James seemed uncomfortable for a moment and then dismissed his apprehension. "Well, before I found you all up in the forest, I was heading up an investigation. The only true concrete evidence was a symbol that was at every crime scene, so I was looking through here to see if I could find it. It doesn't seem to generate any real attention in my circles back home, so I figured why not."

Othia nodded. That seemed logical. "That sounds like a good leap. After all, the data led you here. Perhaps if you told me about the symbol or drew it, I could tell you if I have seen it."

James pulled out a pen from his pocket and turned over a loose piece of parchment. Othia felt a slight tingle in her thoughts. She felt a gentle touch caressing her mind as though trying to shield her from what might transpire over the next few seconds. James leaned over and drew the symbol that had occupied his mind while he was awake—the Greek symbol for omega with a nearly completed triangle in its center. Othia's vision swam as she tried to focus on the image. Something was wrong, but a small voice in her mind told her everything was all right. Othia then shook her head sadly and said, "I am really sorry. I guess I have been working too hard. My mind is completely blank."

James nodded his head in understanding. "Don't feel bad. I have had all the agencies from state to the feds work this, and they really don't have anything, either." He then looked over at Othia's mountain of books and scrolls and asked, "What are you working on?"

Othia looked at him again and smiled. "Looking for a distraction, huh?"

James smiled and nodded. "Yep, anything to flush the nightmares away." The grin did little to make him feel better; however, he was relieved that it also prevented Othia from asking more questions.

Othia looked back at the towering stack of books and sighed. "To tell you the truth, I am not really sure anymore," she said. "You know those big armored guys who keep showing up?" James nodded and fidgeted slightly. "Yeah, I thought you might know them. When Gabriel and I first started on this little life-changing trip, I was told I was going to be responsible for writing a new parable, so to speak, one that would illuminate all the people who are going to be coming to us with the way ahead for our fight."

James nodded. He had heard something like that from Gabriel. He hadn't envied Othia then, and when he saw the weight on her, he didn't envy her now.

"I was given the base of knowledge, and I have the ability to build on it in here. But you know what I found? The existing Bible is on it. Now granted, I admit it is hard to read in some areas, but the message is correct. I thought hard about why the enemy we face wasn't talked about more openly, and I can only surmise one thing. They didn't want to detract from God in the Bible. It also allows the legion to be forgotten about after each dismantling. I won't pretend to understand why the early church fathers decided to ignore the forces of the damned when they created the text. Perhaps it was Lucifer's hand that kept their quills silent, or perhaps a brokered deal with the Father himself to allow mankind to make their own decision about returning to the Father through the Son. I don't know, but that's what people are going to expect of me. My mind is swimming in an ever-changing sea of incomplete information."

Othia sat down with a thump, and James joined her. He leaned back in his chair for a moment and then sat back up. "Perhaps we are looking at this wrong. Maybe you are trying to focus on things that are not supposed to be solved. Look...you identified what people need to know. It really sounds like more of an addition than creating something new. I had a grandmother who once told me something along these lines, and it stuck with me for a long time. She told me a lot of things, but I will spare you the laundry list of her recommendations on life in general. I had asked why God didn't show Himself for us to see. I reasoned that it would be easy for everyone to follow Him then. She laughed and patted me on the shoulder. 'It's all about faith,' she said. There is a very stark difference between knowing and believing. God wants us to believe in Him, to have faith, not to just know Him. Maybe that is what is going on here. You don't need to make people know God, just have faith in Him.

"You have enough information in here to do that. I don't think any of us here are looking for you to give us some new revelation. I know a lot of it will come across that way, since all this is new, but truth be told, you are in this just like we are. Go from works that are already there for the base. It's been good enough for over two thousand years. You only need faith. The rest is a bonus if it provides information that will help us against whatever is waiting for us out there. But start small, and let us all grow together." James watched as Othia smiled, and her eyes began to water.

She leaned over and hugged him tightly, her words a whisper through barely contained sobs. "Thank you," she muttered.

The two sat in silence for several moments, and then James cleared his throat and smiled sheepishly before he said, "If you don't mind me asking, what is the overall theme of what you are tasked with creating...now that you have found your focus?"

Now Othia smiled and said, "I am the one who gets to tell 144,000 people the truth. But even more than that, I have to explain to them the true horrors of Hell to make them understand the repercussions of failure."

James sat silent for several more minutes, and then he smiled warmly again. "I don't think my grandmother and I ever talked about that. But I am willing to help in any way that I can."

Caught off guard by the light hearted tone of the statement, Othia began to laugh, "I might just take you up on that, so don't go too far. Thank you so much, James. I needed that."

Chapter 18
Each of Us is a Spark in the Darkness—Who will See Us Before We Fade into Nothingness?

A student is not above his teacher, but everyone who is fully trained will be like his teacher.
~ Luke 6:40

Location: *Ephesus*

Gabriel stood motionless as he looked at the mound of ancient texts resting on the table before him. The stress of bringing people together and trying to learn at the same time was beginning to take its toll. He walked out of the library and looked around the organized chaos in the main chamber.

They had received additional arrivals last night, and he had been summoned from his sleep by a vision of more people waiting in the clearing. The speech had gone better this time, and there had been less in the way of speculation when the group of one hundred newcomers met the people who had already arrived. Men and women of all backgrounds were filling their ranks; single people along with those who had families, all felt the call. The arrival of families didn't sit well with him. The pain from Jennifer's death wouldn't heal and he didn't wish that kind of horror on anyone. He knew it was pointless to ponder why God had chosen men and women with families, so he simply didn't. One thing was certain: Marie would be elated to see the arrival of twenty children. The collective mood was electric. A seamless bond developed between both groups, and instantly, the new group fell into the fold.

Now came the task of organizing the sleeping arrangements so that the masses could focus on other things. Lost in thought, Gabriel didn't notice the imposing figure that arrived behind him until it said, "There are many things we need to talk about, Seraph."

Gabriel nearly jumped as he spun around to look at the massive Percious looming behind him. Gabriel thought about lecturing him not to sneak around but knew it would do little good. After all, he could have been as loud as a marching band, and Gabriel doubted he would have noticed.

Gabriel's head slumped forward, and he nodded. Percious's voice rang in his mind. "If I might make a suggestion, you need assistance with the sorting of facts here in your halls of wisdom. Reach out to the other legions and see if there is an enlightener available."

The intrusion into Gabriel's mind nearly overshadowed the advice from Percious, and Gabriel paused for a moment to collect his thoughts. "A what?"

"An enlightener, Seraph. They are the keepers of knowledge and hold powerful position within all legions. I understand that Othia is assuming this position for now but is still learning how to truly use all the information. It is a very difficult task. If I am mistaken, please forgive me."

Gabriel's mind began to grasp the meaning of the word, and then he shook his head and said, "No, I think you might be right. That sounds like what I need, but how do I get one? You guys don't exactly carry cell phones, and I don't suppose there is an Internet café in Heaven where you all check your e-mail."

The small attempt at humor was lost on Percious, and the massive warrior simply pointed at Gabriel's belt. Gabriel's eyes and hands followed, and a spark of understanding ignited in his mind as he felt the smooth surface of the cherub stone. "How do I use it again?" he asked.

"That is an answer I do not have, Seraph. Each interface between a cherub and their commander is unique. I would suggest silent meditation to arrive at the solution."

Gabriel nodded, and then looked up at the scar-covered face of Percious and said, "I guess I should get started once everyone settles down tonight. Start with small steps and then see where it leads. What do I ask for? Or rather, who do I tell him to seek out?"

A roar of laughter filled the massive cavern, and some of the new arrivals cast unsure glances in the direction of the imposing angelic figure. "Your cherub is very capable. Some among us would argue that he is the brightest we have ever seen. He will know what to do. He comes from a long line of—you don't know who your cherub is, do you, Gabriel?"

The slight breach in protocol was lost on Gabriel as he simply shook his head. "That is another matter handled between you and your cherub," Percious continued. "I am sorry for breaching the sacred edict and beseech your forgiveness. You should spend time in meditation, Seraph. Your cherub can be your lifeline when all else is lost. Your relationship is essential for your success. Tell him what you need, and the cherub will take care of the rest. He will seek out those legion enlighteners who are appreciative of your allegiance, and should he exhaust all other venues, he will attempt to make contact with those legions who would rather your involvement not exist in this war. Either way, the cherub knows the political fallout of such dealings and will handle all contact with finesse."

Percious looked down at Gabriel and waited for any further comment, but when none came, he cleared his throat and said, "There is one other matter that we need to discuss, Seraph, and it is one that I feel should be addressed sooner rather than later. The security of this sanctuary is critical, and as of now, there is little in the way of combating any enemy elements that could come into this holy area. We need to train and equip your warriors. We need to begin preparing for war."

Chapter 19
Closest of Advisors

My tongue will speak of your righteousness and of your praises all day long.
~ Psalm 35:28

Location: *Ephesus*

Samantha watched Gabriel with the small select group that he had been meeting with constantly over the last two days, and she slowly walked up behind them. As she got closer, Gabriel saw her and quickly motioned her over. She noticed that the small group was completely enthralled with what Gabriel was saying: "We need to start organizing. Over the last few days, you all have come to me as the spokesmen and women for smaller clusters now beginning to take shape in the sleeping area. Some say that there is no greater recommendation of leadership than that from your peers and I have to agree. You all are now leaders within the legion."

The group fell silent. Samantha wasn't sure any of them were breathing. She had guessed that Gabriel had chosen his initial leaders. She just didn't know them. "We are going to begin to separate the legion into different elements," he continued. "I need information, and we need to do this as rapidly as possible. Each of us was chosen for a reason—our skills in life, our faith, and our family lineage, amongst other things. But right now we have a truly gifted pool of people, and we need to start taking advantage of those talents. We need to develop some kind of structure like any other organization.

"First and foremost, I will need a list of the different skills to be annotated and then split evenly amongst all of you. We will look at those who have handled weapons, such as ex-military or law enforcement, those who are trained in administrative areas, those who have the gift of building, whether they are foremen, plumbers, or electricians, and those who are mechanically inclined.

"As to the groups that you are currently in, try to find anyone who has connections with procuring products with money, but under the radar. Once we have the base structure outlined and some semblance of order, we are going to start training. Our guest," Gabriel said, leaning his head toward Percious, "tells me that the damned will soon be able to track us down and will begin to attack.

"The altar in the center of the great room is a gateway of sorts. From that spot, we can travel to and from a great many areas, but it also means that should the damned find out about it, they can get here as well. We need to organize quickly and begin to channel new arrivals into the new groups. There are twelve of you. That means that each of you will have roughly eleven thousand people in the sub-organizations that will branch out from here. We have a little time now to work on systems, but we need to streamline this process, because we don't want to fall behind. I will need one person from everyone's group here to work with me to help me organize this chaos. Please give me someone you would want to keep, now that you know what your role is."

Gabriel stood, and the others followed suit. "We have three days. You are dismissed." Gabriel watched them all leave before he said, "Samantha and Scott, can I talk to you for a minute?" They both stopped and exchanged glances. Gabriel joined them and smiled. "I know that both of you noticed that there were truly fifteen people at the meeting. There are twelve commanders plus myself...and the two of you."

Scott and Samantha simply looked at him, waiting for a punch line of some sort, but when he sat down, they both exchanged glances, shrugged, and joined him. "I know that I cannot do this job alone," Gabriel continued. "Samantha, you have been through more life experiences in these last few weeks than anyone I know at your age. You're young, energetic, and you have a gift for seeing things as they truly are. I know that you are very detail-oriented with your previous profession, and I believe that you have some untapped talent that we desperately need. I need to have a powerful second, should anything come up, and I see unlimited potential in you."

Samantha was speechless and didn't answer, but stared at Gabriel. "Please, Sam; selfishly, I want someone here whom I trust with Marie and whom she knows as well. But even more so, I trust you. I know you can do it."

Samantha smiled and said, "It's not that. I am just amazed that you picked me. I'm a college student, or at least I was. I am not a leader."

"No, you are more than a leader, Samantha. You are now second in command of over one hundred and forty-four thousand people."

Samantha simply sat silently, nodding her head, and Gabriel gave her a warm smile.

"Scott, I know that we didn't get off to the best start," Gabriel said. "I did, however, appreciate your candid opinion when we were gathered together that first night. You have the people's interest at heart, and you were the only one to speak up."

Scott shook his head for a moment and then said, "It was completely out of character for me, Gabriel. I am usually quite reserved in my actions and tend to over think a lot of things before acting."

Gabriel nodded his head and said, "You have a military background, right? I overheard you one night in the sleeping area." Scott nodded, and Gabriel smiled before he continued, "Then I did make the correct decision. I want you to be my third in command. Accompany me on most of the missions and act as Samantha's right hand if I am away and things are going on at the temple here."

He looked at Samantha and Scott and saw the burden of leadership beginning to weigh on them as each began to digest the enormity of the situation they both found themselves in now. Gabriel smiled again and stood up, extending a hand to each of them. "Come on—we have a lot of work to do."

Chapter 20
Essentials

Empires were not built in a day.
~ Good Advice

Location: *Ephesus*

The three days passed quickly, and at the close of the fourth day, Gabriel felt as though things were beginning to take shape. His time was now spent discussing the training regimen with Percious and receiving updates from the new commanders on their infant units. Every second of his day was sought after, however only one meeting placed everything else on hold. Marie's laugh recharged him more than any caffeinated drink or meditation exercise. The sheer delight he saw in her eyes as they played together made it all worthwhile and kept him centered in the evolving chaos.

On the morning of the fifth day, Gabriel was awoken by Marie tapping him on his arm. He sat up quickly, the fog of sleep melting away in an instant. "What's wrong, babe?" he asked.

Marie pulled at his hand and tried to get him to stand up. He rose and allowed her to lead him out of the library. They walked for several minutes. Gabriel wanted to ask what was going on but simply remained quiet. Their steps carried them down to the well, and Marie sat down, waiting for her father to join her. She reached for two pieces of low-hanging fruit and passed one to Gabriel.

Gabriel admitted it was odd behavior for her, but she had been through a lot after losing both Jennifer and Peter. It had taken almost three days for her to stay awake for more than two hours at a time.

Now her face was cheery, but her eyes still held on to a deep sadness. Gabriel took a bite of his fruit and smiled softly at Marie and then said, "What's up, cutie?"

Marie looked down for a second and Gabriel scooped her up and held her in his arms. His eyes met hers, and he could see the beginning of tears welling up. "You miss Mommy and Peter?" His voice was a whisper. He couldn't have asked the question any louder even if he had wanted to, and his own tears began to flow when Marie sobbingly nodded her head. They both cried together for over an hour. Gabriel let Marie's angry fists slam into him as his own voice echoed in his head: *She needs this, and so do I.*

After their hearts began to mend, Gabriel carried Marie halfway up the tunnel, and then she decided walking was more preferred. The pain was still there, but it was different. Marie had taken some of it away. The emptiness was still strong, but his fears for his daughter, which had once compounded his grief, were now slightly diminished. As they crested the final small rise Gabriel saw his commanders standing in a loose group waiting for him. Standing off to the side from the group was Percious, his massive form towering over the rest of the assembled men and women. Gabriel smiled and looked at Marie. "I love you," he said. "Do you want to sit with me in the meetings?"

Gabriel watched Marie's eyes move toward the sound of children laughing. Then she said, "No, thank you, Daddy. I love you." Gabriel kissed her on the cheek and watched her run to investigate what the kids were doing. He saw Samantha wave at him and let him know she would see that Marie was looked after.

Gabriel envied his daughter's joy for a moment and then focused on the task at hand. Scott came up to meet him, and there was a small smile on his lips. "Something funny you want to clue me in on?" Gabriel inquired.

Scott shook his head, "Nice to see you with your daughter is all. I know you have been working late, and I was going to say something today. But it looks like Marie beat me to it, smart kid."

Gabriel nodded, "We needed some time. What's the gathering of the minds all about?"

"Percious wants to start talking through his recommendations for training and wanted everyone in leadership gathered together so that they all get the same spiel, I guess," Scott admitted.

Gabriel felt the weight of leadership on his shoulders, and it began to take its toll. "Fine, a little before I wanted to do this, but okay, let's go ahead and cross this bridge." He motioned for Percious to come over and join the two of them.

The angelic warrior's armored body moved silently over the cavern floor, and he nodded his head in respect when his eyes met Gabriel's. "Seraph, I am sorry to gather your leaders unannounced, but I have received word that we have not heard from my commander. And many in my legion fear the worst. I would like to begin the training regimen sooner rather than later if my services are needed by the leadership of my legion."

Gabriel thought for a moment before speaking, "I was under the impression that Semyaza assigned you to this mission personally. If you haven't heard from him, how are you relieved of the task?"

Percious frowned and shifted under Gabriel's gaze, "I was asked not to divulge this information unless necessary, but now it is proving to be so. I spoke the truth in that my commander assigned me to this mission. My fear now is that his second in command will countermand that order and bring me back within the folds of the Twelfth Legion. I know you are aware that not all of my brothers are as accepting to your involvement in the war as my commander and I. His second in command is one of those who believes that you have no place in the conflict and that your presence is a distraction rather than a blessing."

Gabriel grimaced in disgust, "Well, now that we have that out of the way, let me tell you how I see this going down. Your commander has assigned you to me, and until I state otherwise, you will stay here and accomplish your task. Until different facts arise, a seraph issued the order, and I outrank your second in command. We may not be as large as your legion, but I promise you, Percious, we will be as lethal in time, and your leadership would be wise to understand that—or it will be a costly error on their part. Do I make myself clear?"

Percious's jaw dropped. The threat against his legion was so unexpected that he was not angered, but rather so taken aback by Gabriel's statement that he could only nod curtly and allow the rest of the conversation to play out. "We will begin now," Gabriel continued. "You have my commanders. They are assigned to you. Scott and Samantha will require private sessions, for their services are needed right now for other tasks. If they can make the group session, that is preferred, if not you all can collectively work out the details. Train them well, Percious. I will inspect the training soon. I know I will be impressed. Start with hand-to-hand and close-quarter combat as we agreed. Range-combat training will happen later when we can acquire and modify the weapons we need."

Gabriel looked at his commanders. Their eyes were wide after they witnessed the exchange, and none dared speak. "I assume you all have chosen someone to act as your second in command. Scott will work with them to ensure that all the information requested has been collected. There will be significant changes to our structure while you are training. I expect that you all will stay on top of things, getting updates from your second in command after each session. You all have access to me any time of the day. I'm not going anywhere, and things are about to get very interesting and fast-paced. Keep up and make sure we talk often." With that, Gabriel turned and walked toward the library. There was a lot of information he needed to process, and he was now beginning to see how little time he had. His thoughts went to his cherub. He had taken the advice offered by Percious and meditated with the stone. The results had been mind-blowing. The celestial messenger had departed quickly with his new mission after their brief introduction. Now, however, the cherubs prolonged absence was bothering him: *I hope you can find the help we need.*

Gabriel discovered James sitting in the library, his nose buried in a book, "Interesting reading?"

James looked up, and his eyes blinked lazily, "I guess it depends on what you call interesting. What's going on out there? Looks like the apple cart got a little upset."

Gabriel looked back at the huddled mass of his commanders walking behind Percious as they entered the dark room, "They'll be fine. I think we're going to start playing politics here shortly, and I was never any good at it. How are you feeling?"

James looked away for a moment before he said, "Fine, I guess. Still a little stiff. I can't say that I am getting any sleep, but at least I still have my good looks."

Gabriel smiled, "Well, whatever you tell yourself to sleep better at night. Not to change the subject, but I have a question for you. We need to get some equipment to start making this group of people look like an army. We have an unlimited amount of money, but I need to go under the radar to keep our friends in the government who want me hanged as a traitor and our associates in league with the enemy from finding out about it. Any idea on who can get us weapons and gear?"

James rocked back in his chair, pondering the inquiry. "You sure you want to go this route? I mean, we are supposed to be the good guys. How is buying things from bad guys staying with the status quo?"

"Yeah, I know it sounds a little off-base, but I can't see any other way to go about it. You got any ideas?"

James shook his head, "No, I guess you're right. How do you want pull it off?"

"Get with Scott and Samantha and make a list. We need to get it right the first time so that if we need more, we can go and do small buys and not run the risk of detection. Can you get it done in a day?"

The front legs of James's chair hit the floor, "Man, you really are on the warpath, aren't you? Yeah, I can get the initial contact done and get with Scott or Samantha to make the list, but the hardware will take a little while to get here. But before you tell me again you want it in a day, let me see what I can work out. Money truly makes the world go around, and if there isn't any shortage of it here, we can probably make anything happen."

Gabriel nodded as his mind began to move to the next set of problems he needed to tackle. He shook hands with James and caught sight of Scott walking with three strangers. James chuckled, "How about I link up with him after your meeting? You are one busy guy, brother." Gabriel laughed as well and waved as James departed.

"Shall we adjourn deeper into the library?" Not waiting for a reply, Gabriel led the small group into the far side of the library, which acted as his private area where he could sleep and think without the constant assault of questions. Scott stood silently for a moment and allowed all the newcomers to circle around, and then he returned Gabriel's smile. "As requested, here are the people who have talents in the areas you desired." Scott motioned toward a middle-aged man standing at the far right of the group. He was moderately built and still clean-shaven even after he had been at the stronghold for several days. "This is Steve," Scott said. "He's a contractor and has worked his entire life in construction. Plumbing, electric, building—he has expert knowledge of it. Real smart if you ask me, but he won't let on." Scott smiled, and Gabriel shook the man's hand firmly. Gabriel kept his comments to himself and allowed Scott to continue.

The next person he introduced was a dark-skinned woman, about fifty years old. She was heavyset and looked to be from somewhere in the Middle East. "This lovely lady here, sir, is Lona," Scott said. "She is an information specialist...or rather was in her previous life." Scott shared a smile with Lona and continued, "She has contacts in the computer world and knows the ins and outs of networking. She has some connections with government contractors that could come in handy in the future if we run into trouble. Just food for thought."

A muscular man stepped forward before Scott could introduce him, and extended his hand. Flaming red hair gave Gabriel the impression that the man was Irish, and when he spoke, the thick accent confirmed his suspicions. "My name is Kalub," he said. "I prefer to do my own introductions if you don't mind." His tone was mild, and there was not a hint of disrespect, simply a firm statement of desire.

Gabriel nodded and shook the man's hand, "What do you bring to the war, Kalub?"

The man thought for a moment and then shrugged, "I have worked for several governments and have—how shall I put it—intimate connections that allow people to move unnoticed through commercial travels. I am not a criminal—I state that so we are clear from the beginning. Legitimate government offices have sanctioned all of my work, and while I never asked for specifics, all my customers were always satisfied with the results."

Gabriel smiled and nodded. "Well, Scott, I think you must have read my mind. I was just talking to James about this line of thought, and now it seems we can start to make some serious headway. Since I have you all here, let's talk. I think we are going to make some generous gains with our quality of life."

The meeting soon ended, and Scott watched Gabriel move back toward the library. He could see the weight of responsibility pressing down on Gabriel's shoulders. He couldn't fathom how that man kept going. There were stories circulating, but he had gotten the truth. Samantha had confided in him after their respective places in the legion had been established—their epic journey to the temple, the loss of Gabriel's wife after she turned into some kind of creature. It wasn't fair, yet with each passing moment, he could see Gabriel growing stronger. The retelling of the tale ensured Gabriel gained a lot of admiration throughout the ranks of the newcomers. They all rationalized that their sacrifices to follow God's will were not as severe as what the man destined to lead them had given up. Gabriel disappeared into the library, and Scott turned back to the small group who had just met with him. "Well, we have a very large task ahead. Tell me what you need so I can give Samantha and James our list. I want to get the basics up and running fast. Feel free to work out-of-the-box ideas, but the foundation of our new home is our only focus."

Steve, Lona, and Kalub all nodded in agreement. "Let's meet back in a few hours," Scott said, but he stopped as wide eyes stared back at him. As he turned around, the hairs on the back of his neck began to rise. He craned his neck up, taking in the mammoth armored form of Percious.

Hard eyes looked down at him. "Your position in the legion has been made known," the angelic warrior said. "Come with me."

Scott swallowed hard and stood slowly. Percious gestured toward the dark room. Scott turned back to the small group, and with a slight smile on his face, he said, "We may have to be a bit more flexible on the next meeting time."

Chapter 21
The Enemy of my Enemy is Never my Friend

All sins, no matter how small, still cannot exist in the presence of the Father.
~ Azrael, the Gatekeeper

Location: *Port of Tacoma, Washington, U.S.A*

The tranquil sound of small waves sloshing against industrial shipping docks was lost on James and Samantha as they sat hidden in shadows. Butterflies circled maddeningly in Samantha's stomach. Her new position of leadership was taking a lot of getting used to. Now as the second in command of the legion she was taking her first real step to fulfill her role. James had done all the legwork, and now they were making a deal for real. Samantha felt as though she had gone back in time, just starting at college again, unsure of what the future held. Her pounding heart and queasy stomach made her mind whirl. Things had changed so much for her recently that back at the stronghold she'd been afraid she was growing numb to life. Now she knew better.

Her eyes glanced over at James to find him smiling. His expression was one of good nature with only a slight hint of mischief. "You're so nervous I can hear your heart pounding all the way over here. Relax. This is just the initial meet and greet. No heavy hitters. Just middlemen. Everything will be okay if we play our cards right."

"You mean if I don't throw up on their shoes."

James's smile broadened, "Yes, you could put it that way. Personally, I was going to say turn on your natural charm and let your unique talents help us be successful. We have to set the tone of you doing this alone. I'm fairly certain this level of brokerage isn't vetting us against local police databases, but if we do set something up, the next level will. I'll stay in the shadows for those, but we need to establish you as the main buyer up front."

Samantha nodded and calmed herself. She pulled out a small set of headphones and leaned back against the metal shipping container and began to gently rock back and forth to the beat that only she could hear. Her fingers danced along her leg as though controlling something, but James could only guess where her mind took her to regain a sense of peace before the uncertainty of their situation took over again.

James knew Samantha had the plan constantly running through her head, but somehow talking seemed to bring out the strong personality that Gabriel had said she possessed. James had only caught glimpses of this, but here, hunkered behind a shipping container at the Port of Tacoma, he could see it starting to push forward. It was just the two of them, as the black marketers had specified in the agreement. Black market dealers were easy to locate, but when you wanted large quantities, then alarm bells began to go off. Organized crime is an elaborate and alluring dance. They needed to stay somewhat legit without drawing attention to themselves. Money would help; however, they required the right mix of shippers and suppliers to make it happen, and that talent resided only in the big leagues.

Samantha opened her eyes and saw James smiling at her again. She took out the headphones with her slender fingers, and smiled sheepishly. "Sorry, I guess it is an old habit. Music helps me relax."

James nodded, "I can go along with that, but that isn't like any music I have ever heard."

The large smile brought about a good-natured laugh from Samantha. "Well, this was always a big hit when I would work at the clubs back home. I guess it is just a difference of taste." Samantha saw the wheels turning and started talking again before James could form any conclusions. "I was a DJ for a group of house music clubs in the city my college was in." She felt silly that she needed to justify her use of the word *club*, but she felt the need to make sure James didn't come to the wrong conclusion about what she had once done. It was foolish to a degree, but deep down, she still felt the strong desire to prove herself to her new family.

"Sounds like you have a lot of talent. I am sorry that things have taken a turn for the—well, I am not too sure what this is. Worse? Weirder? Heck, all I do know is my life is totally upside down, so if you came all the way from Europe, you must really be in a spin."

Samantha nodded, "I don't miss it," she said. "I mean I do, because that is all I knew. But doesn't this just feel right, as though we are supposed to be doing this? Now don't get me wrong, not this right now, but holistically—with the legion and all."

James understood, Gabriel had taken him in and protected him even after all the insanity had settled from entering the temple. He was free to come and go as he pleased, and still, he stayed. Something was truly moving inside him, and he knew exactly what Samantha was talking about. It just felt right. James was now really beginning to see how strong the petite and stunning young woman would be in the legion, and now he admired Gabriel for being able to see it so early. "I guess you're right," he said. "Go back to relaxing. We're going to have a long night ahead of us."

Hours passed, and the pair still remained in the shadows of the towering stacks of metal shipping containers. James shook his head slightly as Samantha checked her watch for the hundredth time. "Just relax," he reassured her. "Everything will play out one way or another."

The pair sat in silence as the temperature continued to fall. James stood slowly and began to pace. The cold night air was biting, and any warmth he hoped to achieve would require at least some movement. His eyes caught sight of the headlights a fraction of a second before Samantha's did. He heard her gasp as she looked in the direction of the approaching car. His vision blurred for a moment and then snapped back, his heavenly gift coming to the forefront.

James's mind refused to believe what he knew he had seen. Six strange creatures flew maddeningly around the luxury car. Rotten wings beat wildly as the deformed monstrosities swooped down toward the ground and then raced skyward again. James knew what they were. He just didn't believe it. Samantha had told him a great deal about his gift, and he had learned more from the library; however, this situation still seemed too fantastic.

Pushers—that was what Samantha had called them. The ancient books described them as corruptors, or soul poisoners. All the names fit. These were the bottom rung in the demonic hierarchy—lost souls created in the image of the fallen. Their task was to turn the hearts and minds of humanity away from God, and should a man or woman succumb to their corruptive nature, a black smoke would emanate from the tainted soul.

The pushers hid somewhat in the open, maneuvering humanity's needs above their morality. They could come as a faint whisper in your subconscious, rationalizing away your sins, or an abrupt mood swing making you overly aggressive, their touch always there. Each push on mankind by these abominations caused the armies of the fallen to grow.

Samantha saw the horror etched on James' face, and she whispered one piece of advice before the car arrived, "Pray...quickly."

James' gift was a supernatural ability that had blossomed when he had entered the temple. He had always had a gut feeling about people that always turned out to be correct, but now he could see their true colors too. Even though he had read many tomes in the library and spoken with Percious, he still didn't truly have a firm grip on his gift. His eyes widened at the approach of the headlights. He wished he could turn it off as the burning eyes of the demons looked their way. Fear caused James' vision to flash between his gift and normal sight. The effect was similar to a strobe light, but it added an even greater feeling of fear as the demonic creatures flickered before him.

Samantha had placed a simple symbol at the base of his neck, scrawled in ash. She had said it would keep their allegiance to the heavenly bodies hidden from the pushers. It stood to reason that if they could see the enemy, then the enemy could see them. They had no real way of testing the symbol. They had to rely on the information provided by their forebears to get them in the door.

The luxury sedan slowly stopped in front of them. Certain secluded areas of the Olympic Container Terminal allowed for private meetings like this to take place without any interference from civil authorities. James followed his own advice as he stood calmly and watched six armed men in business suits step out from the sedan. High-pitched squeals and animalistic barks filled the sky as the pushers landed on the shoulders of the men. The fat, bloated, disease-ridden creatures were ignored by their prey; however, their physical presence did not go unnoticed by James and Samantha.

The armed men were obviously not part of the initial agreement, but the meeting was now under way, and James knew if they were to have any hope of success, they had to be very flexible. The group from the sedan paid them little attention as they searched the immediate area to make sure that James and Samantha had come alone. Moments later, a second set of lights appeared. A black limo silently pulled alongside the gray sedan, and the dealer with whom James had set the meeting finally emerged.

"You're punctual," the dealer said. "It is nice to see that common decency is still alive in America."

The thick Italian accent was not lost on Samantha, and she stifled the smile that almost crossed her face. Her mind began to play out the next few minutes, and her confidence grew as their plan fell into place. She met James' gaze and nodded, stepping toward the limo.

She had worked hard to perfect her English over the years. Countless study sessions in Lithuania had made her the best speaker in her college class; however, she now needed to sound nearly as bad as her friends, who had never studied other languages. She needed to make a bond with this man to ensure everything went their way.

"Civility is always in order when large amounts of money are involved," she said. "Don't you agree?"

The black market dealer eyed Samantha, his gaze coming to rest on her toned, athletic legs. His imagination took over as to what lay under the heavy coat she wore. "I couldn't agree more. If I had been told by our mutual friend of your beauty, we could have met at a more comfortable location. My name is Jon Franco, and I am at your service."

Jon Franco gently kissed Samantha's slender hand and then shot James a look, which told him to back away. James played the part of a facilitator and watched critically from a few paces back.

"The pleasure, I am sure, is all mine," Samantha said. "You may call me Aija. As long as we can talk business here, this location will serve us both perfectly."

Jon Franco nodded in affirmation, "Your facilitator stated that you have a bountiful reserve of cash to fund your requests, is this correct?"

Samantha looked out into the shadows as though disinterested with the talk of her finances. "That is true. I do not have cash, as you put it. I prefer not to touch my 'net worth,' as the Americans call it, so I deal in precious metals, stones, and artifacts. Will that be a problem?"

Jon Franco nearly lost his composure, for the potential for profit nearly caused him to salivate excessively. The creatures all took to the sky and began to circle above them as Samantha's eyes caught a slight tendril of black smoke making its way from the depths of the open limo door. Her heavenly gift, like the one bestowed on James, allowed her to see the true essence of each of the men's souls. All of them were marked by pushers—not completely claimed by either side, however, their corruptive influence would tip the balance of the security detail toward darker acts. She knew the pushers kept the men they watched entrenched in sin to keep them loyal to the dark powers until their souls were truly claimed.

Samantha turned back to the dealer, her expression hinting that she was interested again. "My needs are diverse and very extensive. I have been told that you can provide me with everything I could possibly need...for the right price, of course."

Franco nodded again, a large smile appearing on his face. Samantha looked back at the limo and then turned toward Jon Franco, her tone shifting from flirting vixen to offended bitch. "Jon Franco, would your boss like to join us, or does your employer simply like to watch?" Franco's expression faded from unwitting surprise to unease when Samantha did not turn her gaze from the limo.

"I am your first check, Aija. Should my employer, as you put it, find your offer intriguing, then we will have another meeting to discuss the details. This is how things are done."

Samantha turned her salacious eyes toward Franco, and the man nearly came undone. "I like to make very intimate relationships to ensure both sides work to constantly keep the other happy," she said. "If your employer is not interested in meeting me, that is fine; however, I will not meet with anyone other than you from here on out, Jon Franco. The lack of courtesy your employer has shown me has placed one strike in our relationship. Pray there are no further incidents where my patience is tested. I believe we have exchanged enough pleasantries for you to decide if we are to go forward. I would advise you to make your decision quickly. I have many appointments already made for the morning."

Franco frowned and said, "Your over-eagerness is out of place. Perhaps you are police, huh?"

Samantha saw Franco's hand instinctively drift toward his jacket. She shook her head confidently and continued, "It is my experience that the law enforcement of this country is always underfunded. Here is a sample of what business with me can yield." Samantha slid off the leather backpack she wore and handed it to Franco. She masked the strain in her expression so well that Franco nearly toppled forward when she let him have the bag. "Our list is inside with what you may consider as the sufficient funds to make our first order paid in full."

Franco unzipped the top of the backpack and could not mask the expression of greed that took over. He stood again, zipping the bag and smoothing out his suit. Franco bowed slightly. His gentle kiss remained on Samantha's hand until a flicker of headlights brought him upright, a large smile on his face. Samantha inclined her head to the side and waited as Franco seemed ready to burst.

"It would seem your aggressive timeline to establish a deal and proof of purchasing power has impressed my employer. Please pass any future requests through the channels. As for this one, we will get back to you with a delivery date. I cannot wait to begin our relationship together, Aija." Franco walked briskly back to the limo, and seconds later, both James and Samantha were alone once more.

Chapter 22
Sweat in Training so as Not to Bleed in Combat

The waves of death swirled about me; the torrents of destruction overwhelmed me. The cords of the grave coiled around me; the snares of death confronted me. In my distress I called to the Lord; I called out to my God.
~ 2 Samuel 22:5-7

Location: The Schloss, Germany

Silence possessed tangibility, a force within creation few understood. Isolation was key to communicating with things, which preferred to remain hidden in the shadows. Navigating into the abyss through meditation was a proven method. Denying the mind access to the senses while establishing the connection was the secret, which was kept from the masses. All major religions, faith practices, and self-help dynasties understood that there was an essence in all of us. Humanities inner light, soul, energy—whatever you called it, was contained within the body. Yet none of them ever connected the difficulty of transcending into the ethereal realms was because of the body. The senses, which allowed us to experience the world around us, inhibited the mental conquest of reaching out into the depths of creation. The few who stumbled upon the pathway were unprepared for the caress of unimaginable nightmarish abominations and went insane.

This was one of the many secrets the Assembled guarded. Deep within a subterranean warren beneath the Schloss, Uther slowed his breathing. Encased within a custom sensory deprivation chamber he shut off his mind's physical need to utilize his five senses. His slow, rhythmic breathing sounded like a rock concert. As he altered his meditative state, the stillness around him invaded his mind. Bringing his heart rate down he felt the stillness around him shudder. Imagining a gentle breeze blowing from beneath him, his spirit left his corporeal body.

Creation was a fickle animal. For reasons beyond his comprehension the doorway to the dark powers he courted had swung open. He had many speculations, but he held them close. While absolutes were dangerous things to search for, he would proceed cautiously until the way ahead became clear. His abilities had amplified since the summoning of the demonic emissary. While their interactions had not been as fruitful as he would have hoped, her presence alone spoke volumes to the favor in which the Morningstar held him.

Weightlessness in his spirit form was to be expected; however, he ensured to hold a tight mental connection to his physical form to prevent being lost in the darkness forever. He felt a new presence encircle him before it spoke. The silky, smooth voice that surrounded him seemed incredibly old, yet youthful at the same time. "I have longed for this meeting my son. The world is in your hands; soon it will be at your feet. The doorway is open, come through and witness a glimpse of what is to come."

The blackness parted and a soft white light began to radiate above him. Uther relaxed again, allowing his spirit-body to drift further from his physical form. An astute student of mysticism and the occult, Uther was not surprised as his consciences reshaped into his mortal form again. While the flesh contained the soul, they were mirrored in shape and size. So it was logical that his immortal essences would desire to resume its customary form. Uther stood on lush green grasses. The fertile patch of soil sat at the edge of a cliff. Its jagged edge dropped nearly a thousand feet blending into a fertile plane, which extended to the horizon. As Uther looked at the bountiful landscape below the smooth voice returned.

"Nothing escapes my sight. Your loyalty to the true power of creation shall be forever remembered. All that is before you shall bow to your will as we restore the true balance to the world. The dark emissary's arrival marks the beginning. Realities will begin to merge as the prophecies of the final days are fulfilled. Within the words of the past you can see the trails to come. Both kingdoms will begin to display their influence, yet only the conquer shall prevail."

As Uther's gaze remained on the fertile lands before him a gigantic blurred mass appeared on the horizon. A steady wind blew, racing across the lush trees and brought the haze into focus. There before him was a sprawling city. Designed in such a way that the tall, rigid structures complemented the gentle, rolling greenery around it. "To achieve greatness many obstacles must be overcome. However to rule, only one thing must be achieved—cripple or crush my enemies. The masses wish to serve; it is in their collective nature. Those whom are destined to see the truth shall not resist. The huddled few who refuse to accept their place in creation will fall away and be consumed.

Uther listened intently, knowing instinctively that the world he saw before him could be his if he obeyed. His words felt clumsy and off as he tried to convey his conviction to his lord, "My life and soul are yours to shape. You alone heard my cries of pain during my darkest moment and only you comforted me. It was by your touch that I began to bend the world to your desires. I long to sit at your right hand, for only then will I feel complete."

The voice returned with a smile in its tone, "So you shall." Uther watched in silent wonder for a few moments as his aspirations were made manifest upon the landscape before him. Any desire he possessed would revel itself through a new haze on the plains below.

Sensing his deepest yearning, his unseen lord broke the silence, "Humanity has lost sight of the simple beauties of life. Where harvest, homestead and the hunt were their own reward the population of today want more than to exist in the world around them. They want to conquer it. Not out of blind ambition but out of uninformed entitlement. The masses of today don't understand their place. We, my son, shall illuminate them."

Uther stood transfixed, his gaze locked onto the sprawling farmlands before him. The unseen speaker continued on, "To reach them you will have to speak directly to their materialism, their need to dominate in a digital world. Where little matters except the outward appearance of their dreams being within their grasps. Vanity has always been a weakness of some within humanity, yet now it seems to be an affliction that has spread to nearly the entire population. It would seem that in striving for their individualistic need to exist they have collectively left themselves easy to conquer. Much like Narcissus, humanity will succumb to your wishes as it gazes upon its own self-proclaimed beauty."

"In these efforts to shackle humanities perception of reality, I will be there to assist you. Yet even with the impending end soon upon us, the barriers must be weakened. You must gather the harvest. Collect for me their suffering, agony, betrayal, and guilt. For as the walls between the planes thin the prophecies which tell of my arrival will come to pass."

A gentle hand fell upon Uther's shoulder and turned him around. The unseen speaker remained behind him yet there seemed to be a smile in his voice again as he saw the awe in Uther's expression. "We have existed within the shadows for too long, when we emerge it will be as a conquering king."

Before him stood a sea of people, reverently bowed in submission to him. Each figure was silent, anxiously awaiting his command to give purpose to their lives. Beyond the seemingly endless mass of subjects stood an imposing edifice of an Aztec Ziggurat. It's position before him was not as a historical site, but as a seat of power. The voice returned, inserting itself to accentuate the grandeur of the visage before him. "I know you so well my son. You deserve a fiefdom of days gone by. A return to when the realms existed together. You hold humanity by its hand now, steering it to your will. Soon the masses will be at your feet.

"Prepare my son. I am coming soon. Gather the blood of the chosen where the boundaries between planes are thin. First look to the lands where redemption failed and man's own appetites crushed the innocent. Then cut deep into the heart of the self-proclaimed Branch of Heaven to ensure it rots from within. Only as these come to pass shall the secrets I have given you occur."

A wicked grin came to Uther as his gaze remained upon the masses before him. "Your will be done."

Chapter 23

Hidden in Plain Sight

The Lord will punish with his sword, his fierce, great and powerful sword, Leviathan the gliding serpent, Leviathan the coiling serpent; he will slay the monster of the sea.
~ Isaiah 27:1

Location: *District of Colombia, U.S.A.*

Greek inspired architecture surrounded Cincaid. The Basilica felt more like a prison than a church. She was not surprised by the summons. Her involvement in the Chicago projects where four priests died performing various exorcisms had caught the attention of the Monsignor. The Basilica of the National Shrine of the Immaculate Conception was an enormous structure. The largest Catholic Church within the United States, it was the logical location for the team from the Vatican to begin its inquiry.

Monsignor Roberts had greeted her personally when she arrived. The survivors of the Commons incidents, as it was now referred, were revered among the clergy. Mother Superior Genti was at the top of the list. The clergy talked at great length about spiritual warfare yet few truly knew what it meant. The two battle-weary teams that returned from the Commons were now treated like celebrities. The upper echelons wishing to be seen with them, the inner workings of the organizations trying to understand all the events that elevated their peers above them.

The interviews of the clergy and support staff had taken place individually. She was the last. Seated before a group of special investigators from the Vatican she suppressed a cruel grin. Each of the priests was part of the inner circle and bristled with self-importance. One stood apart from the table, he leaned casually against the far wall of the private room in the back of the Basilica. She hadn't caught his name yet, but with such over inflated egos in front of her she would learn the priest's identity soon enough.

Monsignor Roberts opened the conversation. "Mother Genti, Thank you for meeting with us. We know your time is very precious and that you have duties to attend to, so we will try and keep this as brief as possible." The Monsignor and the priest who stood off to the side shared a confrontational glance. Clearly the Vatican representatives did not share the same regard for Cincaid's false persona as the others did. That intrigued her greatly. The global body of the church was compartmentalized in some functionalities. Personal was one such area. Her efforts to infiltrate the body of believers had begun with the Office of Non-Ordained Staff. There her alter-persona was well documented. Not a sudden appearance but rather sporadic interactions, culminating with a steady involvement and then employment. For several years the clergy within the Chicago Archdiocese had seen her as part of the team. Apparently, Rome didn't feel that way.

She waited a fraction of a moment, reading the micro expressions and body language of both men before addressing the senior members of the clergy and the visitors. She kept her voice calm and pleasant as she met each of their gazes, "It is my pleasure Monsignor. I have not been appraised on the final report of the Commons incident, so I can only speak to the limited scope of the event, which I was in attendance. I will answer any questions you have to the best of my ability."

There was a pregnant pause when she finished as the priest, she assumed was in charge of the Vatican team, sat taller in his seat and pondered how to begin. His thick Italian accent accompanied his introduction. "My name is Father Fabio Marco. It is an honor to meet the Mother Superior which has made such an impression upon His Holiness."

Cincaid suppressed the look of satisfaction she felt radiating within her. If she had impressed the upper echelons of the church Uther would be pleased indeed. Father Marco continued, "The church in the new Melina has taken a more direct roll with engaging the enemy. While the ranks of the exorcist orders are still small they are growing and find the touch of the devil all around us. With such a small number of teams they are constantly on the move. Their team leaders have a direct line to the Pontiff if they deem the incident was critical for him to know about. As you can imagine we take all events of spiritual warfare seriously. Especially ones where there is such a large concentration of people affected. Out of the three teams sent in to attempt to drive out the enemy we had many injuries but only your group suffered casualties. Could you tell us what transpired in the apartment? Any details you can recall may allow us to prevent future loss of life if Father Mica did something unorthodox or routine which caused a volatile reaction."

Cincaid smoothed her habit as she nodded her head, portraying an outward appearance of submission and slight timidity. "Of course Father Marco. I had the pleasure of working with Father Mica on several occasions. When I arrived at the Commons the teams had already begun their work..." She described all the events she witnessed entering the Projects. Her descriptions of the exorcism within the apartment was drastically altered, however she was careful not to lay blame or implicate any of the team. Her rendition described an unexpectedly strong demonic entity that caught the clergy off guard with catastrophic results. After she finished each of the priests seated at the table introduced themselves and asked a series of questions. When they finished Cincaid looked at the lone priest standing off to the side. She kept her tone innocent and submissive, "You didn't ask anything Father. Are you one of the exorcists in Rome?"

The man ignored her, however Monsignor Roberts answered, "Father Antium works in a different order within the Vatican. You needn't concern yourself with him. Thank you for your time Mother Genti. May we call upon you again should more questions come up at a later date?"

Cincaid nodded and rose, clearly dismissed. Making a mental note to investigate Father Antium once she departed. As she exited the room her eyes locked on her driver standing at the far end of the hallway leading to the rear rooms of the Basilica. He passed her a folded note, the use of any technology would have drawn attention. She paused as the implications written upon the parchment forced her to suppress a curse.

Recovery of critical asset compromised. Port Angeles harvest site still under investigation by local police. Artifact listed as priority one has been confiscated as evidence. High profile nature of case makes covert retrieval impossible. Please advise.

Composing her anger she readjusted her habit. She motioned for the driver to take her to the car. Cincaid's mind raced as another complication to her plans was heaped upon her. The identity of the silent priest would have to wait. Her fabricated position within the church was secure. The meeting had been more to reinforce the hierarchy of the religious organization, not to assign blame or look for the unfaithful within its ranks. The Willis issues still needed to be addressed, along with other matters. Her personal intelligence gathering would have to be put on hold. She needed to energize other aspects of the Assembled to ensure nothing was overlooked or left unattended.

As she exited the Basilica she could hear her phone ringing in the car. "*From out of the frying pan and into the fire.*" The private muse did little to capture the enormity of the challenges she would have to conquer. However the fire would do more to aid her efforts than hinder her. The abominations in the shadows would see to that.

Chapter 24

Have Faith

So the king gave the order, and they brought Daniel and threw him into the lion's den. The king said to Daniel, "May your God, whom you serve continually, rescue you!"
~ Daniel 7:16

Location: *Ephesus*

They walked in single file, worried expressions evident on all their faces, each of them knowing they were all about to get a true taste of what they had agreed to be a part of. The hulking form of Percious walked ahead of them, his rhythmic pace kept them all in step with a wordless cadence. The small group walked into the dark room. A strange feeling of loneliness and oppression befell all of them, and each fidgeted in their own way to try to cast off the feelings.

Percious pulled at a ring on the floor to reveal a passageway below, leading deeper into the earth. Without a word, his massive form disappeared into the blackness below, the implication that the man in front of the line needed to follow him down, clearly stated. Nervous comments and hushed laughter filled the blackness as each of the twelve commanders and Samantha dealt with the darkness in their own way. The floor leveled out, and they saw a beacon of light coming from Percious's halberd, which he had pulled from his back. Shadows danced over his armored form, and the huddled masses gathered around him.

"Here is where we will begin to train. Where we stand is not only a sacred place, but a unique one as well. Our Creator has turned his gaze from us while we conduct ourselves within this dark room, and his actions make it impossible for any others to see as well. This act, however, has additional effects. What you train on, plan, or execute while within this chamber will occur outside normal reality. Time passes differently outside His gaze. The short time we spend together here will allow your mind and body to possess things in a different way. Should hours pass here, days or weeks will pass within the temple. When you emerge from our training your mind and body will respond as if we had been training that length of time in your reality. This will allow us to cover a vast amount of information and techniques without you becoming disenchanted with the process.

"What I am about to show you has been a sacred gift from the heavenly warrior ranks to humanity since the inception of the Thirteenth. Your actions from this day forward will enable you to be the backbone of this legion. Should you fail, humanity is doomed. Should you master what I am to teach you, your loved ones, along with the rest of your kind who are deemed worthy, will join our Creator and live for eternity within the promised sanctuary of His home."

No one spoke. Percious looked over each of the twelve in turn, his steadfast gaze unnerving some and drawing blank stares from others. Samantha stood apart from the commanders. She shook under Percious's gaze, but her eyes did not turn away. Green orbs stared unshakably at the angelic warrior, and he walked toward her. Towering over Samantha, as he looked down at her, she remained steady in her gaze. As she looked straight up, her neck craned to ensure that she could still peer into his piercing eyes, and she stood trembling. "You do not look away," he said. "A rare quality. What is your name?"

Samantha swallowed and took a step back, her eyes remaining fixed on Percious. Her voice was strong, but Percious could hear the underlying fear in each syllable. "Samantha," she managed.

"Ahh yes, the second in command. I will watch your progress very closely, Samantha." With that, Percious turned and slammed his halberd into the ground, and light erupted in the chamber.

Each of the commanders gasped as they looked across the sea of armored suits resting on wooden poles. Several noticed the lines of weapon racks, which held various deadly creations used over thousands of years. The angelic warrior walked over and stood in the space between the extensive rows of armor and initial set of weapons.

"These have served your ancestors for generations," he said. "Thousands of warriors, who have been tasked from the Son as you have, used these weapons to destroy His enemies. I can tell you that none of them had any more training than you; yet with the help of beings like me, you all will become the fallen's worst nightmare."

He motioned for Samantha to come forward. Her reluctant steps dragged the request out, and soon, she felt foolish for lingering. Percious pulled out one of the armored suits. "Do you know what this is?" the angel's voice boomed in the chamber, and each of the commanders jumped at the question.

Samantha looked at it for a moment. She knew that she was not a scholar. For crying out loud, she hadn't finished college, but she did know one thing for sure: fear in front of this warrior was only going to be trouble. She squared her shoulders and looked at him again, her gaze unflinching when Percious directed his attention toward her. "It looks like the armored suits that knights wore during medieval times. Other than that, I couldn't tell you. What are they?"

Percious thought for a moment and then nodded, "The similarity is correct, but they are only similar in appearance. This is the armor of God. A gift from your oldest ancestors to aid you in fighting the monsters of the abyss. The things you face will be stronger, faster, and more skilled in the art of killing than even the most gifted warrior your legion will possess. This armor, along with other tools, will aid you to hopefully live long enough to make a difference."

"They all look the same size. What if we have people who don't fit the mold?" The question had come from a middle-aged man in the back. His rounded features and graying hair told Percious that wisdom was going to be his greatest asset to his newly formed legion, and not feats of strength.

Percious looked at the man and smiled. Scars from past wars contorted and shifted, and while the smile was genuine, it made several of the commanders grimace. "The armor is blessed and will mold to each warrior. It will not hide girth, only protect it."

The man blushed, and his hands went unconsciously to his stomach, which hung over his waistline significantly. The group chuckled—the jab lightened the mood a little.

"The armor is unique in creation," Percious continued. "It is nearly a living creature, yet lacks a soul, so it is not truly a living being. When you put on the armor, you will feel a sensation akin to millions of tiny hairs tickling your skin. This is how the armor will interact with your body to understand what is currently going on and how it may aid you. Those tiny follicles will embed into your body through your skin without causing you any harm, and you and the armor will in a sense become one. Your entire body must be in contact with the suit for it to work properly. Over time this interaction will allow the armor to modify its appearance to better serve you. What you see now is how your most recent ancestors' bodies and minds molded the gifts. Samantha, please don this suit of armor so I can show your comrades how it works."

She looked at the armor sheepishly for a moment and then spotted a small alcove to the right. Her hands grasped the wooden frame holding the armor erect, and she lifted it to carry it to the alcove and change. Her eyes went wide when the armor nearly flew out of her hands. It weighed nothing at all, yet she felt how sturdy it was. The pieces were large enough for her to put on quickly. As each piece touched her body, she felt a flash of heat, not unbearable but definitely noticeable. It faded quickly, and as the armor cooled, she saw that it had molded to her frame. Her body looked sleek and graceful in it, her brown hair cascading down her back caused a subtle contrast to the drab black that covered her body below her neck.

The attack happened fast. There was a blur of motion from Percious, and she experienced the feeling of weightlessness as she sailed across the room. Her body crashed onto the floor. The thud of the armor was accompanied by the cries of alarm from the rest of the group. She stared up at the ceiling, and soon, she saw Percious's face appear over her. "Do you need assistance?" The question was simplistic but she could hear the undertones of sarcasm, and she pushed his massive gauntlet away. She felt fine, better than fine, actually. As she pulled herself up off the ground, she watched the massive gouge in her chest plate fade away as if it had never been there.

She looked at Percious for a moment and then said, "You could have warned me. I don't think I would have moved, you know."

Percious smiled and responded, "Ah, but where would be the fun in that?" His eyes then shifted to the rest of the assembled commanders. "What you just saw was a strike at about thirty-five percent strength. It will not stop everything, but it will deflect quite a lot. It is virtually weightless, and the blessing from God on the armor itself will allow each of you to be more than you are now. Minor damage can be repaired by the suits quickly, and with prayers, even severe damage can be fixed. These along with other traits make the armor invaluable to warriors on the planes of the damned. That does not mean you don't need the training, but it will allow us to train faster than if we were not blessed with such powerful gifts."

"Is it similar to how fast you and Gabriel moved the first day? I didn't see any armor on him. How did he move so fast?"

The question had come from the portly middle-aged man, and Percious smiled again. "He has been touched. He is part of the seraphim, one of the most powerful beings in all creation. When he dons his armor and fights, you will see the wrath of God erupt from his weapon. Enough questions. Choose a weapon from the racks and don your armor. We start training now."

***

Samantha's body hurt all over. She knew she wasn't the only one, but she didn't care. The training had lasted over twelve hours without a break, and while the armor hadn't felt like it had weighed anything, her body now screamed with every move, informing her that something had weighed a lot. She watched everyone else in the small group. Each of them looked exhausted. How was she supposed to keep up with things that were going on while she was away getting beaten on all day?

One of the newly appointed seconds-in-command was waiting by the entrance to the sleeping area. Before the training had begun, she had met with all the commanders' seconds to distribute supplies. She waved at him, and he scurried over. He was a small man in his mid-forties, and he was losing his hair. "Please tell me good news, Andrew," she said.

Andrew smiled, "This was an easy day here from the looks of what you all went through. We have moved into bunks. Let me show you where you are. I set everything up the way you had it on the floor, so really, it is just a geographic change."

"Did everything go smoothly?"

"Yep, we showed up at the drop spot, and all the stuff was there, so we started making trips."

Samantha looked at the hundreds of beds that had been assembled. "Andrew, how long do you think we were gone?"

Andrew thought for a moment and shrugged his shoulders. "I don't know. Two or three days—why?"

Samantha nearly stumbled and fell. Andrew caught her by the shoulder and pulled her upright. The concerned look on his face told her everything. She put up a dismissive hand and said, "It's all right. I am just tired. Let's see where I am living."

Chapter 25
Those Who Tell Secrets from the Past Bear More Than Just the Tales They Tell

Do not be deceived: God cannot be mocked. A man reaps what he sows. The one who sows to please his sinful nature, from that nature will reap destruction; the one who sows to please the Spirit, from the Spirit will reap eternal life.
~ Galatians 6:7–8

Location: *Unknown*

Gabriel squinted into the maddening mist. Cool water covering his skin left behind a thin film as it quickly dried. It was all an illusion in his mind, he told himself. It was just a dream, and while it was a reprieve from the habitual nightmare of his wife's final moments on earth, there was still a strong sense of foreboding lingering in the air.

The mist began to clear, and Gabriel found himself standing in what appeared to be a city square. Towering buildings of white marble crafted more expertly than anything Gabriel had ever seen before covered the immediate area. The structures were each over five stories tall and seemed to mirror ancient Greek architecture. His eyes settled on an imposing structure in front of him. Hundreds of white steps inclined to the bronzed doors at the top of the beautiful structure. Above him, columns of enormous height supported an ornately crafted roof.

Gabriel was squinting again to see what the artist was trying to portray with the large mosaics on the walls when he felt a presence behind him. As Gabriel turned, he became acutely aware that his sword was not on his back, and his mind raced, thinking where the priceless weapon could have gone. A slight chuckle met his ears a fraction of a second before his eyes settled on a woman in a simple white robe.

"Well, this is our first meeting, Gabriel, and I must say, you are a remarkable individual," she said.

Gabriel frowned as the soft voice soothed his mind. "You seem to have me at a slight disadvantage. Have we met before?"

The woman smiled, gleaming white teeth shone, contrasting with her olive skin. "In a manner of speaking, you and I know each other well. But we can save introductions for another time. There is something you need to see. Something the powers that be are holding from you."

The last word echoed a moment. Gabriel's mind tried to rationalize away the feeling that this wasn't a dream at all. He had felt this way before. Visions of his training from his angelic tutor Vicaro flashed in his mind. The abominations he faced to prove his worth to an unseen collection of would-be judges were fresh in his memory. The robed woman seemed to grow impatient. Her voice filled the emptiness of the buildings around them when she said, "We have things to see—"

Gabriel took a tentative step forward. Something wasn't right, but there was little he could do. His mind told him to let things play out and see if he was right to be concerned. He started up the stairs and regarded his self-appointed tour guide. The woman looked of average build and height. Long black hair gave her a youthful look, but the dark envoy seemed ancient. "What is this place?" Gabriel asked.

She smiled, "Ah...he does know how to question his surroundings. How wonderful. Well, my son, this is the pinnacle of understanding, the epicenter of enlightenment, and the finality of humanity." Gabriel was startled by the last comment, and his guide simply continued up the vast staircase as though she had simply stated that the sky was blue and everyone knew it. "You surprise me in so many ways, Gabriel. You question every facet of authority, their motives, their goals, and their hidden agendas. You have done this your whole life. I find it odd that we are here now and you are so willingly skipping to the tune of authority. Frankly, I expected more...hmmm."

Gabriel took a sidelong glance at the stranger. *Who was this woman?* The hairs on the back of his neck began to rise as unanswered questions began to take on a life of their own. If this was a vision or dream, why was everything so cryptic? All his senses screamed at him that this was not a dream but a state similar to what he had experienced in the pit. But that was impossible. Christ, Semyaza, and Vicaro had all told him there would be no more training dreams. As his mind tried to sort things, his guide appeared inches from his face, a calculated smile etched on her tanned skin.

"I can see the wheels turning, Gabriel, but let's get to the top. Then you are really going to have something to think about."

He really didn't have a choice. He hadn't brought himself here, so he reasoned he wasn't in control. His guide didn't seem to want to hurt him, just show him something. But show him what? The columns grew as he got closer, each of them reaching toward the perfectly blue sky.

The peacefulness felt forced. Something was off. *Where were all the people? Birds, clouds, anything besides the building and this bizarre woman ushering him up the stairs?*

They came to the last step, and the two of them stood in front of a pair of bronze doors. Beautifully etched artwork covered the entire expanse of the twenty-foot doors. It looked like a testament to the discoveries of mankind—medicine, commerce, science, reason, logic, everything humanity held up as a triumph. The illustrations were easy to digest, save for the centerpiece. Whatever carefully crafted work had rested there was gone now. There was no overt damage to the integrity of the edifice, but the intricate design was gone, perhaps destroyed by something. Gabriel looked at his guide with expectant eyes, and she simply shrugged.

"Everyone is a critic, right?" With that, she pushed open the bronze doors. They swung inward effortlessly, and Gabriel stared into a vast chamber. It reminded him of churches he had seen in Italy, vast columns reaching up to the ceiling, flanked by beautifully crafted statues and artwork. This room was at least ten times the size of the largest church he had ever seen, and everything seemed to revolve around one small item on display at the center of the structure.

The artwork and items seemed to honor and celebrate the accomplishments of mankind. Gabriel admitted he had no idea what the items were, and as he tried to get a closer look, his guide cleared her throat and said, "The item we should discuss is there in the center. The rest are of minor consequence." Gabriel ignored her for a moment, trying to decipher the meaning of the structure he found himself in.

Snapping fingers brought Gabriel back around, "You know, Gabriel, I really had hoped your mind would have been quicker. Here I am showing you something of vast importance, and you are stuck looking at accent pieces instead of the centerpiece."

Gabriel frowned and said, "Let's go ahead and state the obvious here, Ace. You still haven't told me who you are. I don't really know how I got here or even if I truly am here. And you want me to focus on one item and miss the big picture. Does that about sum things up?"

A smile crept onto the unnamed woman's face, "Yes, Gabriel, I would surmise that you have assessed things correctly. Humanity has always been enthralled with the next step...the advancements of intellect or abilities. Some cultures call it enlightenment. Others...ascension. Whatever name it is given, it is your kind's next step. Look at what you face. You appear to be the bottom of the food chain. That is what they want you to think. Learn your scripture, Gabriel. It may save you in the end. Your kind is the only one ever created that is in His image. You need to learn how to tap into that kind of resource. Ascend, progress, evolve—whatever you want to call it, you need to find out how to connect with your Creator so that He takes notice. Your kind is the only one who can. It is a unique gift He has given you, and still, knowing this now, you are going to let them lead you around like a child."

She looked around the room for a moment, her eyes darting in all directions as though trying to find the origins of an unheard voice. "Time is short. The very nature of this structure and surroundings can be pondered later. I would like to draw your attention to this item here."

Gabriel noticed that there was still no passage of information; however, his eyes locked on the object suspended nearly a foot off the floor. The object was small, no longer than the width of his hand, and it was spinning at an incredible speed. His guide waved her hand over it, and it began to slow immediately. Gabriel knew instantly what the object was even before it stopped completely. He had used enough of them in his military career to spot a .308-caliber rifle round. There were subtle differences at the base. There seemed to be an extra primer device, presumably designed to push the round faster than normal bullets. The tip of the round was hollowed out and seemed capable of holding something. The final detail that caught his eye was the strange symbol that was inscribed on the bullet casing and the projectile itself.

The symbol burrowed into his mind like a hungry worm would dig into an apple. A faint whisper caressed his ear, and Gabriel found he couldn't move. An odd sensation brought about by the symbol held him in place.

"Strange that you have never seen this, Gabriel," the woman said. "I know you can feel the power of what this item holds. Your ancestors knew of it all too well. With the enormity of the challenges you face, you would presume your so-called allies would make ready all things to ensure your victory in the end. Well, I suppose those who have power know how to keep it, or how would they have gained it in the first place?"

Gabriel knew when he was being baited, but he was now intrigued. What was so important about this bullet? Gabriel knew answers would probably not surface, but he asked the question anyway. "What's so special about it?"

She gave another smile, but this time, Gabriel swore he heard a thunderclap outside. The woman looked toward the doors again and then back at Gabriel. "That is the true question. Perhaps you should ask those you call friends. You would be wise to ensure you are in league with the correct persons, Gabriel. Be careful whom you trust."

Gabriel took hold of the bullet and felt the weight of it in his hand. His eyes locked on the stranger for a moment, then he saw a mischievous spark in the woman's eyes before searing pain began to course through his palm. He screamed, and as his eyes shot skyward, the world swam violently.

A stern face filled his vision. Planes of red dust with a swirling black and red sky opened around him, as the face before him backed up. "Vicaro?" Gabriel asked, his head pounding. "What the heck is going on?"

The angelic warrior frowned. "That was going to be my question to you. You have been sleeping for several hours. Your soul was traveling, and I along with Othia could not find its location. I came to check this plane and found you sprawled out nearly at the entrance to the pit."

Gabriel stood slowly, the familiar sensations coming back to him from weeks earlier when he began training for his new task from God. Gabriel was still asleep, he knew, or rather he was in a state of sleep where his soul could travel and experience events, allowing his body to rest. Vicaro looked frustrated, his eyes conveying the distress the large warrior had been feeling.

Gabriel looked around and sighed. "Well, not much has changed here. How did I get here, Vicaro? What is going on? Is everything okay?" Gabriel's mind began to race. *Had something happened to Marie?*

Vicaro read his body language and relaxed slightly. "Your daughter is safe, Gabriel, as is everyone else at Ephesus. I felt your soul depart several hours ago and hadn't been able to locate you. I spoke to Othia through her dreams, and she has been searching diligently, trying to find a solution. The question remains, Gabriel. Where have you been?"

Gabriel rocked back and forth on the balls of his feet, trying to shake off a feeling of stiffness in his limbs. The red dust was beginning to cover his clothing and exposed skin, and he brushed at it distractedly. "That's the million-dollar question. But here is another. There was someone there. A woman who stated she had many things to illuminate to me."

Vicaro's face darkened. "What can you tell me about her?" The strong lines of distress were very apparent on the old warrior's face.

"Who do you think she is?"

Vicaro noticed the defiant tone in Gabriel's voice and nodded, "Many things are not as they seem, Gabriel. I have heard tales of other human warriors having similar episodes. Their minds, now open to a new reality, were susceptible to manipulation from my kind. That is not to say humanity is weak-willed or that angels are superior, but that is a tale for another time. This situation may seem harmless; however, the second- and third-order effects can be devastating."

Gabriel nodded, Vicaro was right. The angelic warrior stood to lose just as much as Gabriel if he was led astray. Presumably, that is. Gabriel let the memory of the stranger fill his mind, and then he tried to adequately describe his guide. The stranger's face was a blur. Gabriel knew he had studied the woman's features, somehow feeling that it was important, still the mental image he had crafted seemed useless now.

Vicaro remained silent while Gabriel retold the story. Gabriel saw faint flickers of recognition when he described the surrounding buildings and the final structure that resembled a museum. Gabriel left out the information about the bullet and the symbol it contained. He knew it was the reason for the episode, but he wanted to investigate it first. As Gabriel finished his story, Vicaro began to shift his weight nervously. Seeing the massive warrior unnerved did little to bolster Gabriel's confidence.

"Gabriel," Vicaro started, "the bond you and I share is one that interlocks our souls. Should you die, so shall I. All the knowledge I possess is yours to use, and as our minds continue to commingle, you will see improved results in your knowledge. It is not, however, a sharing of current thoughts. That part of our brains is left untethered so that our reflexes and our essence can still remain somewhat pure. So, to put it another way, we cannot read each other's thoughts. What you describe sounds very familiar. I was not at the incident, yet the tale is well known amongst my kind. Your book of scripture tells of the flood God brought onto the Earth, correct?"

Gabriel nodded his head. His understanding of biblical events had grown exponentially, but little was known about civilization before the flood.

"The eradication of life on the planet except for Noah and his family." Vicaro sighed, as though the retelling of this event personally affected him. Vicaro looked at Gabriel with deep sadness, "My life has been filled with war since I was created. I have taken part in countless battles and seen my kind slaughtered by those whom I once called brothers. None of those events match the scale of death wrought upon the Earth during the time of the flood.

"Humanity was blessed with all the knowledge of creation after Adam and Eve's departure from the garden. Their banishment from God's side thrust them into the world, where the Morning Star reigned unchallenged. The progress seen over the last one-thousand years by your kinsmen does not compare to the grandeur of civilization before the flood. With all their advancements, humanity began to turn to their own talents instead of God to accomplish the things they needed in life. The error in judgment and action of sin rest squarely with humanity; however, they are not the only ones to blame.

"The Morning Star corrupted their ideology and dependence on the Father. Even with Adam and Eve still living, tangible persons who could attest to the glory and wrath of God, humanity still strayed from the path. When only Noah and his family remained faithful to the Father, they were spared. Holy messengers were sent to bring humanity back under the laws of God, but they were slaughtered, the taint of corruption spreading like a virus, making the earth another plane of Hell, where humanity was its demons.

"Thousands of angelic warriors lost their lives trying to reverse the false teachings of the fallen. Their acts of love and compassion were met with violence, ultimately dooming humanity to their fate. The city you described sounds similar to the epicenter of sin. A city so beautiful it could conceal the corruption that rested just beneath its surface. Mankind worshiped their own accomplishments above those of God and soon lost faith altogether. Humanity was judged for their transgression, and all their corrupt knowledge was lost forever."

Gabriel sat for a moment. Everything rang true, and he didn't doubt any of the information Vicaro was divulging. "Why not allow their history to remain...to show how vengeful the Father is, to avoid another disaster?"

Vicaro nodded and responded, "There were many who shared your sentiment, pushing for a way to constantly remind humanity of their corruptibility. Ultimately, it was denied. Only the slightest information is permitted to be given. The birthright of free will prevents the entire story from ever being completely understood.

"Writings and artifacts were rumored to exist, but all tales of tragedy are saturated with stories of items being hidden away for those of the future to find. The past is over, and nothing remains of it, Gabriel." Gabriel held his anger in check. He was getting tired of being treated like a second-class citizen. For all the grandstanding that humanity was the chosen creation of God, they were not treated as such. The past might be over, however he wasn't one to easily forget or forgive.

Samantha's harrowing ordeal in Purgatory, the violent battle to protect his family, the ultimate loss of his wife and son, and the ever-present reminder that humanity wasn't good enough in the eyes of the angelic legions justified his frustration toward the ever-expanding complexity of his task.

Vicaro and Gabriel sat in silence for several moments. Gabriel's mind raced with the knowledge he now possessed. It made sense now. His guide had shown him the violent aspect of that society. Now the question remained—*why?*

He knew that Vicaro knew more details, but Gabriel was comfortable with his current level of understanding. He found it interesting that his angelic mentor didn't mention any of the weaponry that had destroyed God's emissaries. Was it because he didn't know specifics, or because humanity was deemed too high a risk to create those weapons again? Perhaps his guide had been right. Were those who openly called him friend truly his allies? Gabriel looked around before speaking, "Well, I think we have lingered here long enough. Unless you think we should stay?"

Vicaro shook his head. "No, we should get back. We have much to do."

Gabriel's vision became blurred and then snapped back into focus, the beautiful blue eyes of Marie mere inches from his face. A squeal of delight brought Othia running back into the library. Othia's eyes opened wide as she saw Gabriel hugging Marie, small tendrils of dust falling from his clothes. "What...where have you been?"

Gabriel looked up and smiled, Marie's arms still wrapped around his neck. "That is a very loaded question. One I think you will find the answer to very interesting."

Gabriel pushed off the ground while he held on to Marie and sucked in a pain-filled hiss. His eyes darted to his hand, where he saw the outline of a bullet with a single strange mark burning into his flesh. He clasped his hand quickly as Marie tried to investigate her father's source of pain. Gabriel held Marie's squirming body in his arms as Othia gave him a bear hug, her eyes asking the thousands of questions her mouth couldn't articulate. Gabriel nodded and said, "Let's get something to drink. We have a lot to talk about and investigate."

Chapter 26

Truth is Overrated in the House of the Damned

Wealth and power abound and are yours for the taking...all you must do is follow the true rulers of the world...
~ Gospel of Babel 14:22–3

Location: Ephesus

Scott looked at Gabriel sitting, again buried in the library, and frowned. He knew the personality. He had seen it in the army and civilian life—the tormented alpha-male, usually afflicted by his own drive for perfection. In Gabriel's case, however, it seemed complicated, "You look a little worn, and not that I would expect anything else, but some are starting to notice how aloof you're becoming," Scott urged.

Gabriel looked up, "Aloof?"

"Well, we're all trying to start something here, and you seem only connected with the group when it's business time."

"I'm sorry. I guess I missed the grand opening of the coffee shop. Come on, Scott. Get to the point."

"Okay, okay, you know Nick, right?"

"Who?"

"The guy who was an army chaplain before showing up here."

"I thought his name was something different."

"Well, yeah, he goes by Nick since he kind of looks like some movie star. Anyway, he's been leading some services, and it has really helped a lot of us. Your lack of attendance is starting to get noticed."

Gabriel didn't know whether to laugh or to scream, "We're on the brink of war, and you're concerned about my attendance at church?"

The rise in Gabriel's voice caused Scott to raise both hands in mock surrender, "No, not at all. This entire thing is some sort of holy mission, right? It's just drawing some questions as to why the guy at the top who talks with angels and can see demons and all that isn't at the services or even coming to the group prayers. Nick is even working with Othia to do some baptisms similar to what John did in the Bible. Look, I'm on your side, boss. I'm just passing along a tone I'm picking up."

Gabriel sighed and said, "Okay, that's fair. Nothing is ever as cut-and-dried as it seems. I always thought the big picture was black and white; good and evil on this scale had to be polar opposites and that would make the way ahead crystal clear. It's more of a gray area, Scott, and I'm not really sure how to interpret or even really articulate it. I guess what I'm trying to say is I'm trying to figure things out before I have a lot of people looking to me for guidance."

Scott saw the undercurrent of stress in Gabriel's features, "Okay, sure, I'll smooth things out. You want me to send Nick to see you anyway? Just to talk?"

Gabriel shook his head, "No, but thanks."

"You just got to have faith. At least that's one thing I have learned since walking in here."

Gabriel nodded, "True, but you'll all get to the same place I am soon enough, where not only do you have faith but you also know. I know He's up there, Scott. I just don't feel like He's paying too much attention."

Scott was about to keep pressing when Gabriel raised his hand, "Perhaps more later, but we have company." Scott turned to see Othia standing in the doorway with Samantha. The expression on their faces made Scott feel as though he needed to be somewhere else right away.

Gabriel watched Scott leave, gave him an encouraging wave and nod, and then turned to face Othia and Samantha. "Well, you both look as though you have discovered something dreadful. Let's try to keep things in perspective here. Everyone is still safe, so keeping that in mind, what do the two of you need to tell me? Well, don't keep it bottled up. You might explode. Let me hear it."

Othia sat across from Gabriel, and Samantha stood a few paces back. Like a patient diplomat, Gabriel waited to hear the next dilemma he would have to solve for the collective group.

Chapter 27
Evil Knows No Limits

As soon as they were red-hot he commanded that this spokesman of theirs should have his tongue cut out, his head scalped and his extremities cut off...
~ 2 Maccabees 7:2-9

Location: Frankfurt International Airport, Germany

The special luxuries were lost on the occupants of the heavily modified VC-9C executive jet. The lavish seats, the polished wood trim, and the solid-gold accents were the true embodiment of overindulgence. Uther sat rifling through a stack of papers held within black folders. Seven in all, they held the current information on each of his most sensitive endeavors. The sixth folder was open on the table in front of him.

Uther sat with a phone to his ear, his free hand tapping at the photo on top of the stack of papers. A woman's voice came softly over the line, "Sir, I sincerely apologize. The director is on his way. I personally delivered your message, and he is only moments from joining you on the line."

The scowl on Uther's face melted away. "He is a busy man. I am very appreciative that he could spare a moment to receive this information." His voice was like pure silk. The woman on the other end of the call sighed with an unsolicited desire to do anything for Uther.

The NSA—National Security Agency—was a resource in which the Assembled had embedded themselves since its inception. While the leadership of the Assembled always remained hidden from view, their total control of the intelligence agency was complete. Each of the world's covert government agencies was infiltrated by the secretive cabal. Uther would never openly control any of the groups. Control from behind the scenes was more appealing and satisfying.

This was but one of the many talents he possessed, one that had aided him in advancing his empire and developing his connections, which allowed him his independent operations. Muffled voices told Uther that the man he sought was not at his office. Secure communications were wonderful; however, the system often limited where calls could be received. A monotone voice eventually came over the line, "Hello, this is Director Fillmore. How may I help you?"

Uther's grin was feeble as he leaned onto the desk before him, "Director Fillmore, we have never had the privilege of meeting one another, but we share a great many friends. I came across some information you may find useful. My prototype interceptor, the handheld model, has produced some unusual conversations that I thought should be relayed to the proper authorities."

The "Raven" was a non-evasive receiver of communications between any two sources of equipment. Uther's operatives were very fluent in utilizing the handheld devices, but as far as organizations like the NSA were concerned; these game changing systems were still in the test phase. The man on the other end of the phone cleared his throat, "Your message to my assistant said it involved Gabriel Willis, is that correct?"

Uther's smile widened at the excitement he heard in the man's voice, "That is correct. The information collected does not match his vocal patterns; however, the details discussed do show he is establishing a base of operations in the Washington state area." There was a long pause as the information sunk in. All of it was fiction—the phone calls, the photos, and the testimonies from other terrorist organizations. All the groups listed were receiving military hardware shipments from Uther's factories in Europe, and all the players on the video and audio feeds were employees within Uther's companies.

"Director Fillmore, you will find the information in your secure email. I would hate to be presumptuous, but we could help in tracking vocal pattern matches. Our systems are not strong enough to cover the complete spectrum of communications; however, their capability could be bolstered." Uther could mentally see the wheels turning as he heard keystrokes and mouse clicks in the background.

Director Fillmore came back on and said, "This was collected with the Raven system? Impressive. This is viable information. Thank you, sir. I will pass Mr. Willis's name to the front of the target list in the vocal recognition cell. We have installed the newest software upgrades to allow us to monitor all communication means. Do you still have assets observing the target?"

Despite his excitement, Uther's tone remained even,, "No, our internal assets have lost all contact with the target. We are looking at several leads; however, my teams will only be able to identify. They are not staffed or equipped to capture. My agents have validated the 'weapon of mass destruction' threat from this group, so I would advise extreme caution. Eliminating the target is the only way to ensure a disruption of their operations. Once we have confirmation that the threat is gone, I will push my assets to locate the rest of the group before they can reorganize."

Director Fillmore was quiet for a few moments, and Uther willed his mind to remain calm. "The data here states the terrorist cell is only ten to twelve people. Is that confirmed? There isn't a sanctuary location?"

A slight tone of disbelief rang in Director Fillmore's voice. Uther concentrated, a trickle of sweat rolled down his face, "Our sources state this is the top of the leadership ladder. We will recheck with our operatives in the field to ensure that the organization will topple if the head is cut off. The data still supports the need for the target to be eliminated, along with those who accompany him."

"I think we will ascertain that your findings are sound, and target elimination will be a relevant course of action. Thank you for your help in providing this information, sir." The phone clicked off, and Uther flipped through the folders once again.

He took a steadying breath and closed his eyes for a moment. The dark voices that always kept him company soothed his anxiety.

The director would do his bidding, or he would be replaced—that was the very nature of things. His eyes re-opened and glossed over the current reports compiled by Cincaid.

A folded piece of paper was placed on his table, and Uther absent-mindedly picked it up. The stewardess of his plane held many positions—everything from trip planner to expert chef in the small galley and executive assistant. Her slender hand had passed a simple reminder that the ambassador of Ghana to the United States was patiently waiting to meet with him. Uther took a long swig of water and refocused his breathing so as to compose his best smile. With a weak nod he passed the black folders to the stewardess.

Moments later the Ghanaian ambassador sat before him. Uther plastered a charming grin on his face and said, "Thank you for accepting my hospitality, Mr. Ambassador. I know how busy you are, and I hope we have accommodated your needs."

Kind, weathered eyes looked back at Uther. "As always, Mr. Jander, you never fail to impress," the ambassador said. "I would have been delayed for quite some time if you had not allowed me to join you on your private plane."

Complications at the Frankfurt International Airport caused by agents of the Assembled had prevented Ambassador Agaku from flying to his embassy in the United States. Uther graciously offered his open seating to the ambassador, his aide, and one security person. "Please call me, Uther. It was an opportunity that I couldn't pass on. I will be frank, Mr. Ambassador. Your president is difficult to get hold of, even after all that I have assisted with."

The lack of reaction to his comment told Uther how the rest of the discussion would go. He wondered why he should even continue if the end was so clear now. A smile filled his mind's eye—now, where would be the fun in that?

The ambassador sat quietly for a few seconds, then sat a little straighter before he said, "I am afraid we will not be completing our order with your company. My president sincerely apologizes for any inconvenience this may have caused, but we will not be purchasing the military hardware shipment, or any additional training. Our country needs the money spent elsewhere."

Uther's offended expression would allow the rest of the situation to play out as he anticipated. He pressed a small red button on the bottom of the table with his index finger, and his grin widened, "Oh, I think there must be a miscommunication. Keeping your order in limbo on my assembly lines has cost me dearly. I received personal assurances from key members of the president's staff that this was a cemented deal."

Ambassador Agaku's expression darkened. "We are all aware of your influential touch in our government. Apparently, my president doesn't wish to tolerate external influences any further."

Uther smiled again and depressed the small red button a second time. Two nearly inaudible pops signaled that his stewardess had used her Glock .22 caliber pistol with a silencer to eliminate the ambassador's aide and security detail. When she arrived behind Ambassador Agaku, Uther nodded and continued, "Well, Mr. Ambassador, perhaps I should pass a message to your president through you as to how unsettling this news is to me."

Ambassador Agaku, clearly not aware of the deaths of his aide or security detail, shrugged his shoulders. "I would be happy to deliver any message you have; however, I must inform you that my president is very adamant on this decision."

"I am sure he is—"

The ambassador grimaced for a moment as a needle punctured his neck, and then he relaxed as the drugs injected into his body took hold and plunged him into the black veil of sleep.

Smelling salts eventually brought Ambassador Agaku back to his senses. Uther sat across from him, still smiling—but now enjoying a cigar. The ambassador looked in horror at the nylon rope that secured his body to the leather seats. His eyes lingered on his hands, which were affixed to the edge of the table.

"It's superglue. My handiwork, I must admit. Oh, don't worry about the mess. I'll just get a new table when we're done here. I bet you're wondering why I glued your palms to the edge of the table so your fingers are sticking straight up. Well, it's uncomfortable, isn't it? And truth be told, your backing out of our deal makes me uncomfortable."

The ambassador's eyes were wide, yet still defiant. Uther was impressed. There was still a measure of poise and finesse about him. Uther knew it wouldn't last.

"The decisions of my president are his own," the ambassador said. "I am but a humble messenger. If you shoot the messenger, how can you pass communications to my president?"

Uther chuckled. "Oh, you misunderstood my intentions. You thought I was going to shoot you? That is rich. No, I agree with your sentiment, and I know that through you I can pass a very pointed message to your president." Uther then pulled out a pair of stainless steel poultry shears and placed them on the table. The light of understanding dawned on the ambassador's face as he looked at his exposed fingers. For a moment Uther played with the cigar he was still enjoying, and then used his lighter to reignite the tobacco. "That is the only problem with a tightly wrapped cigar. Sometimes you have to keep working at it to get the proper effect."

While terror began to mount on Agaku's face, Uther sat back. His mind took in the man who was the current focus of his anger. At this very moment they couldn't be more different. Uther knew, however, all too well what life was like at the bottom of the ladder. His past kept him grounded. Painful memories gave him a raw focus that allowed him to understand how the world came together. Uther's mind harbored a distaste of tangible pleasures. Life's palpable pleasures quickly lose their allure. Nearly two decades ago the true power of the universe had found him. Broken, frail, and standing at the edge of the abyss—the voices had remade him. Their gifts were greater than any fleeting pleasure; for in pain we covet only the things which aide in our survival. Among the masses, the human eyes lust after beauty, and the flesh hungers as well. These are only there to distract us, to cause our destines to blur. For those blinded by simplistic noble notions their true potential fades away altogether.

Without a word of warning, Uther snatched up the poultry shears and clipped off the ambassador's right index finger. A howl of pain filled the cabin and then shifted to muffled grunts of torment after Uther cauterized the wound with his cigar lighter. "You bastard!" the ambassador called. "This will solve nothing. We don't have the money. He wants to build state-of-the-art hospitals and a competitive school system. We have no need for your stockpiles of weapons!"

Uther leaned in, his pleasant demeanor never fading. "I don't care about the money. I have things, which need to transpire in the West Africa region. Your president's hindrance will disappear. Your population will wither, but don't worry Mr. Ambassador you won't be around to see it." Another clip, and screams filled the cabin again. The fit of pain passed into a lull as shock began to take root in the ambassador's body.

With tears streaming down his face, the ambassador looked at Uther, hate filling his eyes. "Torturing me will not change my president's mind. I can try to talk with him again, but only if you let me go."

Sobs now wracked the man's body. Uther reached across the table and patted the ambassador's shoulder. "That time has passed, but I have faith in your ability to convince your president. When he sees what I am willing to do to one of his trusted advisors, do you suppose he will think about the safety of his family?"

"You won't get away with this. People will know who did this to me. My government won't stand for it!"

Uther sat back and thought for a moment before he started again. "Now how should I tell you this? Well, there isn't a soothing way, so let's just get to the details. I can't wait to see your face. As far as the world and your government are concerned, you departed from us when we stopped to refuel in London to complete other meetings that you had scheduled. Tower logs, car services, and several witnesses will confirm this, and while your president will know the truth, the rest of humanity never will."

The ambassador's face turned ashen, and another snap sent him thrashing in his chair. His convulsions were so strong that his right hand tore free from the table. A second injection to his leg silenced his screams and halted the flapping, half-skinned hand. Uther rose slowly, the façade of pleasantries fading from his face, a look of bloodlust taking its place.

"Strap him down tight and tell the pilot we will delay our landing until after I am finished." Both the stewardess and Uther's security guard set to work. Uther smiled at the thought of the screams of torment, the cries for mercy, and the pleas for a quick death he would soon hear. No one ever truly understood an artist, and only the inhabitants of Hell appreciated Uther's art.

Chapter 28
If Knowledge is Power, How Powerful are Those Who Hold the Truths Behind the Knowledge?

The Lord is a refuge for the oppressed, a stronghold in times of trouble.
~ Psalms 9:9

Location: *Ephesus*

Visions of his dreams clouded his thoughts again. James walked silently through one of the passageways to get back to the main chamber. The dream was always the same, the woman dying in a rushing flood of blood and pain. His sleep was always short-lived because of it, and with the added workload from Gabriel now, he felt as though he never slept.

Each time he had the nightmare, he felt a growing mental connection. He knew her face. He just couldn't place it. As he walked, he tried for the hundredth time to figure out from where he knew this woman. The walk was a gift of sorts, a way for him to sort all the information in his mind. Just today, he had taken the walk five times, exiting the massive door at the passageway's end to make several phone calls and then moving back into the safety of the sanctuary. He continued to make arrangements in Samantha's name while she was in training. This kept supplies coming in steadily while still holding her at the front of their imaginary criminal empire.

The silent passageways helped exorcise his nightmares and organize the massive operation he found himself co-leading. It seemed like an eternity ago when Gabriel had asked him to find them supplies through less than legal means, all in the name of staying under the radar. It seemed a little odd, James thought, but then again, all of this did. The first days were easy. James deflected the complicated supply issues while he got whatever he could to ease the living conditions of the stronghold for the multitudes that were arriving. The numbers were around 350 now, 200 of these so-called saints and 150 family members.

His efforts to avoid Gabriel's questions about the weapons he had requested had worked so far, but he knew it was only a matter of time before that subject would surface and he would have to make more progress on it than he currently had. He enjoyed working with Gabriel, but James truly couldn't tell what their relationship was—in the long run, that suited him fine. With each passing day, James saw Gabriel grow stronger in leadership, and soon, there would be no question why he had been placed in a position to lead.

That didn't mean that he always agreed with their leader. The weapons issue was one area where they sat at opposite sides of the table. The large quantities he wanted couldn't just be acquired no matter how much money you had. There were federal offices that were involved here, and those guys never looked kindly on weapons being moved without their knowledge. James was so lost in thought that he didn't notice the figure standing at the end of the passageway. He came to an abrupt halt when he felt a hand on his shoulder. As James turned to his left, he saw Gabriel's smiling face. *So, the conversation is going to happen now?* James thought.

"Any news?" Gabriel smiled and then walked next to James as he continued his way toward the central part of the main chamber.

"Tons," James said. "Now it's just the logistics of getting the gold to them and the goods to us. I never thought I would be a logistics guy. I never thought I had the attention to detail for it." They both laughed and walked in silence for several minutes before James continued, "I know why you're here, Gabriel, and I don't have any other news about the weapons. I don't know how to get them here without us getting into a big mess of trouble." He looked at Gabriel and was surprised to see him smiling.

"I was wondering when you were going to talk to me about it. I found another way around it. We can get the weapons legally. Well, sort of legally...and then move them here. There is risk while they are in transport, but it is minimal. One of the newest arrivals owns a gun store in Texas. We can order as much as we'd like, and by the time the federal government finds out, he will be here with us...and so will the merchandise. What do you think?"

James smiled and said, "That is so simple. Why didn't I think of it?"

"I think we both know why, James. You don't like the idea of getting them illegally, and I appreciate that. You're right, of course. It would risk too much for not enough payoff. I just wish you had come to me sooner, so that you wouldn't have had to think about dodging me so much."

James smiled warily, "That obvious, huh?"

Gabriel nodded and said, "Listen, we're all new to this, so if there's something that you think is going to get noticed, tell me. We all have different areas of expertise, and right now, I need your help so we can stay off the radar. I need your counsel, James."

Gabriel's hand gripped James' bicep hard as he tried to steady him. James' head lolled back and then snapped forward. His knees buckled, and Gabriel had to bear-hug him to keep him from collapsing. Gabriel gently lowered him onto the floor, and he looked around and spotted a few of the new arrivals staring at them. "Don't just stand there," Gabriel said. "Get me some water from the well and a few pieces of fruit...now!"

They scurried off, not really understanding the request; however, others were soon helping them, and a small group began to crowd around James and Gabriel. James' eyes flew open, and he focused on Gabriel's concerned features. "Well," he said, "this is slightly embarrassing."

Gabriel smiled and responded, "Happens to the best of us. Looks like you could use some sleep and a few bites to eat. Your color is all off."

James nodded slowly, his head pounding and his shoulders slumped, "I don't think sleep will help. The food might, but not sleep."

Gabriel looked at James, puzzled, and shook his head, "I haven't slept well since I got here," James continued. "Well, to be honest, since I woke up in the library chained to the desk. The work has been a great distraction, but all in all, I don't think I have slept for more than a few hours each night."

Gabriel looked around at the gathering crowd and said, "Thank you all for your concern. He's okay. Please go back to what you were doing."

The onlookers didn't wait for any more instructions and began to dissipate quickly. They all shared concerned looks with one another. The story of James's encounter with the first arrivals to the temple had been a well-circulated one. While it was embellished in some areas, it remained true enough, and Gabriel knew that would give many people cause not to trust James. Gabriel helped the police detective sit up. James moved incredibly slowly, as if his entire body was off-balance. The two sat for a moment while James caught his breath and his equilibrium came back.

"James, I have been thinking about something I want your honest opinion on."

James looked at Gabriel for a moment and then nodded his head, "Okay, shoot."

Gabriel took a deep breath and started, "I want to insert you back in the police force. You can get vital info for us that we need to stay ahead of the people who are against us." James sat quietly, and Gabriel continued on, "This will allow Matthew to get back for a proper burial, and maybe we can put pressure on the group doing this to us. Even if it's just biting at their ankles, it's something. You have done wonderful work here, but I think we need this. Percious can help you with your gift so you can spot the enemy before they spot you, and Samantha should be plugged in enough to pull off all the setups for the buys, right? It's a huge risk, so I want honest feedback here. What do you think?"

James remained silent and digested this new development, not only the task but also the way back into the fold. He had been in the middle of an investigation when he had met Gabriel. Now he was most likely listed as missing for weeks. He had used Samantha to do all the meets for the equipment, so there was minimal risk there. It was going to be a tough sell, no doubt about it. He was going to need to look the part of being injured in the woods for weeks. This was going to hurt.

There were several gasps behind him, and Gabriel just ignored them. With the influx of new people each week he simply blocked out the collective reaction, picturing a small group clustered in awe around one of the impressive tapestries.

"Gabriel, there is someone here to see you."

It was Scott. The two had grown close, and he recognized his voice immediately. Gabriel looked at James for a moment, their eyes meeting, and James nodded, "I think you are going to want to take this one, Gabriel." The sheepish grin on James's face sparked Gabriel's interest, and he stood and turned around.

There, standing in the center of the main chamber, was a new angelic warrior. Gabriel looked at Scott and said, "Stay with him. He needs to get some food and water before he tries to move again."

Scott nodded and said, "Yeah, have fun with this one."

Gabriel turned to meet the new arrival. The warrior was different from Percious, taller and more imposing. A familiar pull echoed in his head. "I found what you requested, Seraph," it said. "Please proceed with caution. He is here under orders not of his own choosing." Gabriel smiled to himself; the mental connection with his cherub would take some getting used to.

He looked over his shoulder back at Scott and said, "Big fella, huh? Well, I'd better not keep him waiting." As Gabriel grew closer, he saw a small group of people who had just arrived crowded together, kneeling before the angelic warrior. Gabriel's voice exploded into the chamber, "On your feet!" he demanded. "You are sons and daughters of the Father. You kneel before none except God!" His words echoed, reaching into every corner of its massive expanse. The anger in his voice caused several of the newcomers to jump to their feet and cower away. The others watching from afar saw the fury in his eyes and backed away rapidly as well.

Gabriel felt his blood boil in anger as he approached the angelic warrior. "Well," said the seraph.

"My name is Harrod. I am an enlightener within the Third Legion."

Gabriel stood rigid and silent as he glared at Harrod until the massive warrior knelt before him.

"My apologies, Seraph. I forget myself sometimes."

Gabriel nodded and extended his hand. "I am honored to have you here, Harrod. I am surprised to see a warrior from the Third Legion. I was sure we didn't hold a special place in Abaddon's heart."

Harrod stiffened at the use of his legion's seraph's name, "You misunderstand my place in the legion. I am embedded within the ranks of warriors, that much is true . While we do take orders from them during times of combat, I belong to the cast of illuminators, and we exist separate from the legions. We are the keepers of the written past. I am not here under the orders of the Third Legion's seraph, but rather at the request of my immediate commander, Montif. In our unique position, we are afforded certain additional tasks at the behest of our leadership."

Gabriel heard the tone of cynicism in Harrod's voice, and held back the inclination to send this pretentious, glorified librarian packing; however, he knew that if this was who the cherub had brought, then there was very little to choose from. "Please... this way. I am sure there are other issues that need your attention as well, so I will not delay in telling you our problem." Gabriel then led Harrod toward the library.

As the two walked, Gabriel looked at Harrod's armor and noticed it was a stark contrast from Percious's. The angelic trainer's garb was battle-tested, the scars of many wars evident on the highly polished metal, it whispered its tales of sacrifice and courage as one gazed at it. Harrod's, on the other hand, was a canvas of art. The swirling text that was on all the angelic armor and the black armor of Gabriel's legion as well was present, but there was something more to it. It didn't move but rather blurred itself out. Gabriel had the fleeting impression that the armor thought he wasn't intelligent enough to understand its inscriptions, so it made its images elusive. He knew that feeling was ludicrous, but nevertheless, the thought was building within his mind as they neared the library.

"If I may be so bold, Harrod, why did you allow my soldiers to kneel before you?"

Harrod's misstep was slight, and while it was almost unnoticeable, Gabriel caught it and smiled. "It was not long ago that we were revered by your kind. We were seen as the messengers of God and treated with a reverence that has disappeared in your modern culture. I did not know if your desire was to reinstate old traditions within your legion, Seraph. It is not my place to correct, simply to enlighten."

Gabriel shook his head. This was going to be an interesting project. He took a deep breath and entered the library. Othia sat near the rear of the room, mountains of parchment and stone tablets flanking her slumped form. Gabriel smiled at the sight of her. She was always like this—a true beacon of knowledge lost in a sea of information. Othia looked up and smiled at Gabriel. They were all fatigued, but Othia's eyes held a seemingly endless depth of energy.

She stood slowly and stretched as Harrod's massive frame rounded the shelves. Gabriel's smile widened, and he nodded, calming Othia instantly. "I would like to introduce someone who has come to help us sort out this massive pile of confusion."

Othia's eyes lit up like a child being told Santa Claus was en route to meet her personally. Gabriel moved into an open space between several stacks of leather-bound books to allow Harrod and Othia to meet. The library was cluttered and cramped for someone of his size, yet the armored warrior moved with ease. Othia extended her hand, and Harrod took it gently while he went down to one knee, "It is an honor to meet the thirteenth disciple. I, along with my order, and countless others, anxiously await the parable the Holy Spirit will craft with you."

Othia smiled, the surprise of her unknown title fading quickly as she gestured for Harrod to rise. "You're too kind. I would be eternally grateful if you could help me bring order to this chaotic mess of information."

Harrod's face was a mix of reserved pride and excitement, "Of course, my order is the keeper of our past. We are often not sought out by the legions of humanity to aid in their quests for knowledge. I have been tasked to aid you however possible. If this is your wish, then it shall be done."

Gabriel slipped by Harrod and waved to Othia, "Looks like you have things well in hand. Let me go and check on James and see what everyone else is doing."

Othia saw the smirk on his face and knew Gabriel was escaping so that he didn't have to deal with the uptight arrival, and she couldn't blame him. She knew he was struggling with information overload as well, but his list of priorities was far longer than hers at the moment, so she silently agreed to establish a connection with this new angel. Though how that would happen was beyond her. Harrod looked expectantly at her, and she spread her arms wide and said, "Well, where shall we begin?"

Chapter 29
Man has Always Feared the Darkness. Why Now are we so Unafraid of What Lurks in the Shadows?

Lord, guide my hand as we wage war on your enemies, protect us as we follow your will through blind faith.
~ XIII Legion benediction

Location: Ephesus

Days turned to weeks as their training continued. Each time Samantha completed a training session and emerged from the dark room, days had passed. While she could see the lessons beginning to show positive results, the weariness in her body screamed for a respite.

With each passing session, the main hall began to change. Samantha loved to explore the temple in her very brief free time after the sessions to see what supplies James had picked up in her absence. After her second training session, a medical area was established, and a small computer node was set up. After her third session, indoor plumbing had been erected with showers and working toilets. There was only cold water from the well chamber, but it felt heavenly. Time seemed not to matter down in the depths of her new home, but with each splash of the cool water on her skin, she felt rejuvenated.

There were whispered rumors of modern weapons coming in. James had hinted about a plan for acquiring a large shipment of weapons during one of their talks between sessions, however the details were very sketchy. Absently, her hand scratched gently at the skin behind her right ear. Similar to a tattoo, its permanent presence still perplexed her, and she couldn't bring herself to leave it alone. Her gift from God had been passed a different way, and with this new angelic rune, her perception ability was expected to double. Percious and Gabriel had asked for all the commanders to willingly submit to the indelible rune being placed on them. Both of them tried to explain the need for it, and each failed to sway every commander.

There were whispered complaints that it was too strange to be branded like cattle. The conversation carried on for over thirty minutes, and in the end, neither Gabriel nor Percious swayed them. It was the new arrival, Harrod, who inspired them to take the angelic symbol. The promise of no pain and his recounting of how humanity had worn similar tattoos since the dawn of the legions, enabling them to see the Morning Star and his forces for what they really were, spurred them forward.

However, Samantha knew the final point that solidified it for them all was when Harrod pulled back his right ear and the rune on his pristine skin flared with an inner light. The power within the symbol was unmistakable, and each of the commanders began to see how there would be many mysteries that they would be exposed to, not all of them needing to be avoided.

Samantha looked around at the legion's commanders as they stood in the center of the dark room and waited for Percious. His imposing form filled the stairwell soon enough, and he smiled at the assembled masses. "It is good to see all of you walking and present," he said. "I was afraid after our last session that some of you were going to turn in your newly bestowed position of authority for something a little less demanding."

Their last session had been truly brutal. Not only had they conducted hours of the normal drills of reflexive weapon application, but they had begun to spar. The latter was taxing, given the mental and physical demands earlier in the lesson.

"Today, we begin with practical applications," he continued. A hushed whisper fell over the room as they looked at one another. Percious moved to the side, and Samantha, along with the rest of the commanders, gasped. There standing in chains behind Percious was a bloated form of a creature. Its jaws, which were disproportionally large, were filled with razor-sharp fangs. It also had powerful, hooked claws that it used to pull at the chains securing it to the floor. How had she missed it when they had come down?

The creature rocked back and forth, white foam cascading out of its mouth onto its rotting body. The beast examined each of them with hate-filled eyes.

Percious looked at the leaders for a moment, mentally assessing each of them in turn, their reactions to the creature a telltale sign on how they would react to the initial demonstration. "Samantha, come forward please."

Samantha found her feet obeying before her mind could truly rationalize what events could transpire by walking forward. "This creature before you is called a genoush," Percious told her. "It is a foot soldier. On the battlefield, you will face thousands of these at a time. If you examine the creature closely, you can see that while its jaws are distorted, they are incredibly strong."

Percious accentuated his point by allowing the creature to lash out at his armored forearm. They could hear the armor protest as the creature's jaws clamped down. The massive warrior grasped the creature's upper jaw and pulled hard, and the demon relinquished its hold on his armor. "This creature's bite is worse than its bark. It will make no sound at all, and each of them can act autonomously on the battlefield. The claws are razor sharp and carry a toxin that, if it touches your flesh, will cause it to rot. To give you an illustration, it is like your plague that ravaged Europe. What was it called? The Black Plague. Once one is infected, it will spread like wildfire. But this creature is not without a weakness. Samantha, you will find that weakness and show it to your peers."

Her mind became aware of what was happening only when the sounds of the chain holding the creature in place began to snake free as it lunged at her. Reflex took over, and her sword came up and blocked the creature's claws. She threw herself to the side, rolled, and came up gracefully a few feet away from the creature, steadying herself. Her eyes scanned the genoush as it inspected its new prey.

She watched as it moved right and left, shifting its weight. It lunged at her again, but she parried the blow with her sword. The creature's massive jaws snapped shut on air to her left as she moved nimbly away. She fought to bring her breathing under control. One of the first lessons was to master your own body, and right now, hers was trying to run wild.

The creature didn't allow her to think for long. It came at her again, its claws held high, its jaws snapped rapidly. Samantha rolled and slashed at the creature's exposed legs. It stumbled as black blood spilled onto the floor. The genoush didn't stop, but rather lunged more aggressively at Samantha, its hooked claws scraping against her chest plate. She moved her head to the side at the last second before its massive jaws could close. Instead, it latched on to her armored plate around the back of her neck. She could feel its corrupt breath, and she thrashed her body back and forth to try to throw it off. The creature's claws continued to slam into her armored body, trying in vain to pierce its blessed shielding.

Samantha looked at the creature and saw that its black orbs were still staring at her. Its head, which was attached firmly to her armor, left its eyes exposed and unprotected. She deflected another swipe of the claw, and then with her free hand, she plunged her fingers into the creature's eye socket. She could feel the armored glove puncture the creature's eye, and then spurts of blood and gore spewing out told her she had wounded it. Still, it thrashed. She struck the other eye, and the creature still blindly fought on. The genoush's attack was now less threatening and focused. Samantha struck the beast's head with one hand and drove her sword into its stomach.

The creature's spasm lasted for a minute and then it lay limp. She dropped her sword onto the gore-covered ground and pulled at the creature's jaws as she had seen Percious do only moments before. Dropping it to the ground she looked at it for a moment, and it began to stir. Her booted foot came crashing down and split the creature's skull with one strike, spilling its black and yellow brains onto the stone floor.

Silence filled the air for a moment, and Samantha had the distant feeling that she was alone. With a shimmer, the world around her changed, and she saw a darkness fade away that she hadn't noticed earlier. There standing in a circle around her were the commanders. Percious stood outside the ring, smiling confidently. She had seen that smile before. It was one fathers held only for daughters when they accomplished something only a parent could believe possible.

"What did you learn, Samantha?" Percious's voice boomed in the chamber.

She swallowed hard and tried to get her breathing under control before she spoke. "The creature has strength and some minimal skill; however, it knows no fear. It will attack even when weak and will expose its vulnerabilities unknowingly. It can be beaten, if you focus and strike first. If not, you will be occupied with a burdensome irritant instead of commanding."

"Well spoken," he said. "Are there any questions? None? Good."

Percious then regarded the class as a whole while the creature began to regenerate. "Who's next?"

Chapter 30
Corruption of the Flesh Leads to Corruption of the Mind

All this I will give you, if you will bow down and worship me.
~ Matthew 4:9

Location: *The Schloss, Germany*

Waves of heat filled the large inner sanctum. Thirty candles in thirteenth-century candleholders put off enough heat to warm a large cathedral, however, Uther, sitting behind the large wooden desk, still felt a chill run down his spine. Massive tomes scattered on the floor indicated his search for an elusive piece of information.

Frustration filled his sweat-covered face as he turned at a faint knock on one of the walls on the far side of the chamber. "Enter," was the only word he uttered, and though it was said barely above a whisper, the lone figure on the other side of the bookshelf heard his summons as clearly as if they were in the same room. Uther, who was hunkered over an enormous and ancient text, did not turn as the wall swung in; a hidden door allowing the newcomer access to his private chamber.

Clad in dark, form-fitting clothing, Cincaid entered and stood perfectly still ten feet from the desk and patiently waited for her master to acknowledge her. "You came for something? Cincaid, pass your message and be gone. I need to be alone. It will be coming soon, and there is little time for formalities."

Cincaid stiffened as she noted the fear in Uther's voice. She had never heard him show the faintest concern for his safety until now. That fear penetrated deep inside her like a cancer, "My lord, your acolytes have confirmed success with the mark. They, however, have not found any new information on the location of the temple. There are several leads they are working; however, they cannot offer any timelines as to the success of the task you have put before them. The location you requested has been sought after for nearly three-thousand years, and no one has ever found it. What do you wish of me?"

The question hung in the air, and Cincaid held her breath, waiting for Uther to issue some kind of new directive. He had secluded himself in his private study immediately after confirmation that the members of the Thirteenth Legion had slipped into Ephesus and now the entrance was gone. No one could explain it. Throughout the towering stacks of historical texts, no one could account for the access point being there one minute, and then even after enormous holes had been torn into the ground by over one hundred demons, there was no sign of it.

Cincaid stood silently, watching as Uther's piercing eyes tore through the pages of the large book in front of him. He stood quickly and then slammed the book down. Wild eyes looked at her, and she took a step back. Uther walked toward the hidden door and whispered to himself.

Cincaid knew better, she remained perfectly still and listened intently. His needs far outweighed her own. "I need time to sort out the information in my head," he said. "Cincaid, call the circle together for me. I will be in my bedchambers. Come get me when things are prepared. I can see only one way out of this. This debacle will cost us dearly, and if I elude the inevitable punishment for our failure, we risk losing the gift our lord has sent. If I accept the punishment, I fear the mission will be lost, and we will watch our promised new world fade quickly from our grasp."

Cincaid didn't answer. There was no need. Uther knew his words were law. She watched as he vanished into the shadows and then hurried off to accomplish the task set before her.

***

Dark robes shifted as the frail form they enshrouded moved hurriedly down the hall. An ancient and forgotten text was cradled in the wearer's dry and cracked hands. He was one of the select, one of Uther's acolytes. Truthfully, he never felt special until he put into perspective how the three thousand of his brethren were held above all of the other within the Assembled, where matters of antiquity were concerned.

He had taken a private jet and then an insufferable three-hour ride in a maddeningly fast convoy of six black SUVs to escort a vital piece of information to his master. Padded steps carried his withered frame deeper and deeper into the substructure of the European sanctuary. The man knew of five structures all over the globe. He had never doubted his own limitations of knowledge, but the staggering amount he did possess always gave him pause. Societies had organizations that existed underground, that was understood. This one, however, he could track back to before the false Father had sent his Son to try to take back humanity from the true power in existence.

His thoughts faded as he approached an unblemished gray door. A slight sound off to his left brought his head around to examine the noise. As the shadows drifted back, his frail heart nearly stopped. He had never met the woman before him. The stories he had been told failed to capture her beauty and visible undercurrent of lethality. "Klafa, your age has slowed you. I hope for your sake your news is worth the delay you have placed on our master's schedule."

Klafa nodded his hooded head and said, "My apologies, Mistress Cincaid. The head of my order required a full summation of my findings before I departed. The loss of her left eye and hand has made her more attentive to the actions of our order. Your lesson has been very illuminating to us all, mistress. We are all attempting to better serve our master's will."

Cincaid simply stared at him, the memory of Uther's orders to deal harshly with the head of the acolytes coming to the forefront of her mind. She had spared the woman's life. In hindsight, it had been more trouble than it was worth. Time would tell for sure, and right now, there were important matters at hand. The door swung open as

Cincaid slid a magnetic key against a small strip on the frame. Ushered into a small chamber by a soft breath of stale air, each stood before a pair of retinal and DNA scanners. The equipment was set into the rock, nearly unnoticeable.

Cincaid could get away with using the most technologically advanced equipment here, but inside her master's chamber, Uther still allowed no technology, except in the rarest of circumstances. The slight gust of air filled the small room with the smell of incense, aged parchment, and a very faint undercurrent of blood. The odor would be lost on most, but Cincaid and Klafa were sensitive to such things.

Klafa had only one previous meeting with his master and marveled at how similar the main building and even this chamber were to the sanctuary where many of the Assembled resided in North America. There were subtle differences. Many of the volumes on the ancient shelves surrounding the room were different. The blank walls were covered with tapestries. The two Klafa could see showed demonic creatures all bowing to one in the center of their amassed group. The deformed monstrosity held up a blood-drenched, ancient text. There were subtle differences, but the themes were identical.

The third tapestry was hung behind his lord, and while he didn't doubt it was the most impressive in the collection, he dared not look in the direction of Uther without being spoken to first. The acolytes dealt in antiquity, and many tales surrounded Uther's rapid rise to power. He was said to have unspeakable talents in the dark arts. Klafa knew that some of these supposed gifts had been embellished; however, he was not about to experiment with his own life to fulfill a simple curiosity.

Cincaid brought them two lavishly decorated chairs. The massive desk his master sat behind was crafted from one solid piece of wood and then coated in blood to allow the suffering of the victims, whose life essence covered the entire desk, to energize his master during long periods of study. The pair stood stone silent as Uther continued to read from an open parchment scroll. His hands traced the document as his eyes processed the information.

Seven minutes passed. Uther finally looked up, a slightly displeased look on his patrician face. "Yes, acolyte, you have something to tell me?"

Klafa raised his eyes and met Uther's gaze. He immediately wished he hadn't. The stern look was enough to unnerve him; he was confounded by the flames that seemed to dance in his master's eyes. Klafa stammered, desperately trying to get his voice to work.

Cincaid closed her eyes for a moment and then asked, "Acolyte, what is the progress level of the offering?"

Klafa's focus snapped back into place, breaking his mind from mental paralysis. "My lord and mistress," he said, "our collection of the offering is still progressing. We have adjusted some of our numbers and rituals to compensate for...recent losses." Klafa waited to be reprimanded for bringing up the recent defeat of the Devourer. When nothing happened, he hurriedly continued, "Our records indicate that from the last attempt on the gate 'til now, we have collected eighty-percent of our projected needs. Our effort to stabilize the Commons as a new collection site has shown favorable sings of taking root."

Klafa had been tasked with overseeing the ritual slaughter for the appeasement of the firstborn and the fallen. Since the most recent failure of the fallen's attack on the Gates of Heaven over 346 years ago, his order was amassing the required sacrifices to enable the lifestreams to be opened again. There were rules and risks of societal backlash that prevented the acolytes from simply collecting all their needed sacrifices in one setting. They also didn't want to attract attention before it was time, and a mass ritualistic killing of over 666,000 people would definitely be noticed. The growing need for sacrifices used in other rituals compounded the situation further.

Uther sighed and said, "Please tell me you are not wasting my time with this. You ask me to hold off the gathering of the inner circle of the Assembled and my dark arts for a damn progress report!" Uther's hand slammed down onto the table.

Klafa jumped. Out of the corner of his eye, he could see that Cincaid had not. "My lord, my apologies. I have come with vital information from the head of my order."

Uther sat impassively as Klafa set the massive book on the table. He pulled open pages that rarely felt the touch of mankind. The ancient book's spine cracked loudly, and Klafa turned the pages slowly. He paused and turned the book to face Uther. Klafa swallowed hard and looked up at his lord, "With the recent information correlated and compared against that which our ancestor's agents have recorded, I believe we know how to access Ephesus."

At the mention of the temple's name, Uther reoriented his entire attention onto Klafa. The old man fidgeted under Uther's hard eyes, "Explain! What have you uncovered, acolyte?"

Klafa cleared his throat and then began, "Using the entry point your agents discovered, along with the other three we know of, we speculate that the temple is here." On an ancient map, Klafa's finger rested on a place to the northwest of the United States. "To be more specific, Washington state. We know that the temples have a pure running water source, along with countless entry points. This location makes the most logical sense."

Klafa continued quickly as the presumed slight to Uther's intelligence rang in his ear, "There is one final piece of information. We are still receiving a signal from a beacon. It is very faint and challenging to pinpoint; however, these difficulties are normally experienced when there is an enormous amount of obstructing material."

Uther had lost interest in Klafa's briefing, his mind poring over the ancient map. He knew of the area that the acolytes were singling out. The ancient records indicated the strongholds that supported the Thirteenth Legion were incredibly large. If the location was accurate, then he could see how they would continue to go undetected. Uther raised his eyes and locked his murderous gaze on Cincaid, "Gather whatever you need. All of our resources are available. Dig out the rats if need be. I don't care if you have to blow up the entire area!"

Uther composed himself again and slid the massive book effortlessly toward Cincaid. Her clear, brown eyes looked at the map. *Fitting,* she told herself. *Mount Deception seems like the perfect place to hide followers of the false Father.*

Books of the Thirteenth Legion Series
Book 1- Defiance

Book 2- Awakening

Book 3- Sacrifice

Book 4- Gathering

Made in the USA
Columbia, SC
20 June 2017